SECRETS AND SKELETONS IN THE TEASHOP

PENNY TOWNSEND

Copyright © 2024 by Author Penny Townsend

All rights reserved. No part of this book may be used or reproduced in any form whatsoever without written permission, except in the case of brief quotations in critical articles or reviews.

This book is a work of fiction. Names, characters, businesses, organizations, places, events, and incidents are either the product of the author's imagination or used fictitiously. Any resemblance to actual persons, living or dead, events, or locales is entirely coincidental.

About the Author

Penny Townsend lives in Hampshire. Her first book, Faye Lantern, and the Search for the Village Murderer, is her debut in the world of mystery genre writing.

As a qualified Life Coach and Counsellor, she has a unique perspective on our human qualities, which shines through in the characters she creates.

Penny usually sits in her hanging chair surrounded by colorful cushions, sipping tea from her cat mug while trying to keep her lovable and clumsy dog from knocking the cup over with his tail.

But most often, you'll find her at her desk, writing the next in the series of the Faye Lantern Mysteries.

CONTENTS

About the Author 3

Chapter One: Mr. Penny 7

Chapter Two: Gwen 12

Chapter Three: The Grand Opening 16

Chapter Four: Bill Green 22

Chapter Five: A Rare Bird 26

Chapter Six: Mrs. Penny 29

Chapter Seven: The Invitation 34

Chapter Eight: Grimmer Point 39

Chapter Nine: Hidden In Plain Sight 43

Chapter Ten: The Letter 49

Chapter Eleven: Terrance 53

Chapter Twelve: A Disturbing Turn of Events 57

Chapter Thirteen: Mrs. Field 62

Chapter Fourteen: Under Suspicion 65

Chapter Fifteen: A Shocking Revelation 68

Chapter Sixteen: Drink Up 70

Chapter Seventeen: Patricia 73

Chapter Eighteen: Missing Without a Trace 76

Chapter Nineteen: An Unexpected Friend 80

Chapter Twenty: The Cottage 83

Chapter Twenty-One: Desperate Measures 86

Chapter Twenty-Two: Childhood Memories 89

Chapter Twenty-Three: Finders Keepers 93

Chapter Twenty-Four: A Chance Encounter 96

Chapter Twenty-Five: Hollow's End 99

Chapter Twenty-Six: The Shack 105

Chapter Twenty-Seven: Buster 108

Chapter Twenty-Eight: The Last Time 112

Chapter Twenty-Nine: Felicity 115

Chapter Thirty: Sabotage 121

Chapter Thirty-One: One Step Behind 127

Chapter Thirty-Two: The Spaniard 130

Chapter Thirty-Three: Race Against Time 137

Chapter Thirty-Four: The Storm 142

Chapter Thirty-Five: Nowhere to Run 145

Chapter Thirty-Six: Gone 149

Chapter Thirty-Seven: Done For 154

Chapter Thirty-Eight: Elizabeth.. 157

Chapter One:
Mr. Penny

Daniel had been careful to lead Faye through the front door, completely bypassing the tearoom on the side of the Old Station House. Buster bounded over as they walked in, spinning in circles as fast as his body would let him, his tail wagging just as quickly as she bent down to pet him.

"I'm pleased to see you too!" she laughed, holding him at arm's length, avoiding having her face washed from his frantic licking.

Daniel had already prepared lunch, and as she stood back up, her eyes glanced across the table.

"You really *are* a godsend."

He sat down and flicked his napkin out before placing it on his lap.

"I like to think so."

His mouth creased into a smile as she sat down.

"It's good to have you back. Everything was so quiet without you here — not that I'm complaining…."

He screwed up his eyes, wincing as her smile faded, robbed by her mind as it lurched to the evening Greg had abducted her and taken her to the canal. She clenched her hands tight into a ball and shook off the memory, her hands trembling as she reached for the serving spoon.

They were halfway through their meal when the doorbell buzzed, making Faye jump. Daniel stood up quickly.

Secrets and Skeletons In The Teashop

"I'll get it!"

He made his way to the door, returning with Inspector Rawlings, hat in hand. Faye noticed his eyes scan across the food on the table.

"What a pleasant surprise, inspector. Would you care to you join us?"

She gestured with her hand for him to sit down on the seat next to her. He turned to Daniel, who was already pulling out the chair for him.

"Impeccable timing, as always, inspector. Please take a seat."

"Well, in that case, I don't mind if I do."

Wasting no time, he piled his plate high, unaware of a potato rolling onto the tablecloth. Faye scooped it up, placing it on an empty plate. Small details mattered to her right now. Everything needed to be ordered for her to regain a sense of safety.

"How are you feeling now, Miss Lantern?" And as though answering his own question, looked at her and smiled, "Glad to be home, no doubt!"

Daniel glanced at him, hoping he wouldn't mention the skeleton they found in the walls of the tearoom. But he no sooner had the thought when the inspector stopped eating and turned to Faye.

"I thought you should know—we have discovered the identity of the skeletal remains that were boarded up in the tearoom walls."

Faye fixed intently on Inspector Rawling's every gesture as he spoke.

"They belonged to Mr. Penny, the man who used to live here."

A chill moved through her as Daniel said aloud, "Well, that's creepy!" after seeing the look of horror on her face, his jaw clenched anxiously. "Sorry Aunty Faye, I was just …Well.."

A half smile crossed her mouth. "It's okay Daniel. I agree. It is creepy."

After a brief pause, his eyes lit up, "But what a great selling point for the tearooms."

Faye and Inspector Rawling both turned and stared at Daniel, who froze with his fork full of food in front of his mouth.

"Or maybe not," he said, realizing it was time for him to go. He pushed his chair out and stood up, leaning in to kiss Faye on the cheek.

"Don't worry about the dishes. I'll do them when I get back."

He bid goodbye to Inspector Rawlings, who nodded, and pulled out a folded piece of paper from his top pocket as Daniel disappeared.

"We found this piece of paper with the body concealed inside the lining of Mr. Penny's jacket."

Unfolding the note, he handed it to her. "I wondered if you could shed some light on its meaning….. as you are in the Old Station House…. You might have noticed something here that might give me a clue?"

The letters B.E.G. were written in bold and she was just as stumped as the inspector.

"That's odd? Is it an acronym? Of peoples' names?"

He shook his head, "My men have asked in the village, but nothing came up to link the initials to anyone."

Secrets and Skeletons In The Teashop

Faye turned the note over in her hand, her finger running down the edge of the paper.

"This has been torn from a book."

He nodded as she said, "The letters could be a secret code; something he wanted to keep other people from knowing about?"

He scraped a curl of butter from the dish, placing it over the last spoonful of peas on his plate. "Possibly. But what would old Mr. Penny want to keep secret?"

She shrugged. "I wonder where the rest of the book is?" she said as she passed him the note back. The inspector placed his knife and fork down. He tucked the note back inside his jacket pocket and turned his attention to her.

"This has been an unexpected pleasure, spending lunch with you today," his smile disarmed her, and she relaxed for the first time since she had been back home.

He stood up and placed his napkin on his plate and continued, "If you are well enough, perhaps you could think about what I've said… in case something turns up."

His blue eyes connected with hers and made her catch her breath. Blushing, she looked away.

"I will, inspector."

He hesitated, as if going to say something, his hands clutching tightly around the brim of his hat, before he finally said, "I'd best be getting back to the station then."

He put his hand out to stop Faye as she pushed her chair back to stand up.

"Please don't get up. I can see myself out."

Penny Townsend

He nodded, "Good day Miss Lantern."

And strode out the door.

Chapter Two:

Gwen

Gwen sprinted out of the bakery door on the other side of the street as Faye crossed the road. She rushed forward, arms open wide, to greet Faye with her usual beaming smile, and Faye prepared herself for the inevitable bear hug.

"I'm so glad you are up and about again," she said, finally releasing Faye from her grip.

Faye dusted the flour from her coat as she stepped back. "Thank you. It's good to be back home."

Gwen looped her arm through Faye's. "Have you got a minute? I wanted to have a quick chat."

"Oh, well. Okay." She realized Gwen was already leading her through the bakery and into the kitchen.

"I've just made a pot of tea."

Faye looked across the table. A plate of freshly baked biscuits sat next to a china teapot and two cups and saucers as though Gwen knew she was coming. She looked up quizzically at Gwen, who was still smiling.

"It's Friday! You always walk back from the post office around this time."

"Ah," she nodded. Her eyes drifted to the green and pink cushions dotted along the bench seats on either side of the table as Gwen lifted the woolly sheep tea cozy from the teapot and poured out the tea. Faye took her coat off, placing it on the wooden bench as she sat down.

"I've had an idea!" Gwen said, pushing a cushion to one side as she sat down. "I thought you might like some help with decoding the torn note."

Faye couldn't hide the surprise in her voice. "The note?"

Gwen sipped her tea calmly and pushed the plate of biscuits nearer to her.

"The one that was found in Mr. Penny's coat." A knowing glance crossed her face. "He used to order the cakes for the tearoom from me."

"Of course," Faye said in realization. "The inspector asked if you had any idea who the initials might belong to, as you were familiar with him from the past."

Gwen's eyes danced with excitement. "Yes! And if you ask me some questions, we might work it out. Like a puzzle."

Gwen stared wide-eyed back at Faye. The red scarf, tied around her head in stark contrast to her blonde curls falling out from under it.

Faye could see the look of anticipation clinging to her face as she waited for a reply.

"Well. I don't suppose it will do any harm if you were so well acquainted."

Gwen clasped her hands together and let out a squeal of delight. Fidgeting in her seat and getting comfortable, she pushed at the back of her hair, straightening her headscarf.

"SOOO.... As I said. Every morning, Mr. Penny would come over and pick up the cakes and scones for the teashop. He always had a laugh and a joke with me and Tina, the part-time girl." She stopped, her eyes moving up and back in contemplation.

Secrets and Skeletons In The Teashop

"He was a ladies' man, for sure," she continued as her face lit up. "Perhaps he had a jealous lover who murdered him? Or she was blackmailing him, and he wouldn't pay up anymore?" Her excitement was barely containable now.

Faye realized how gossip could so easily spread around the village and interrupted her. "You're reading far too much into a simple flirtation, Gwen. Tell me, did he work in the teashop every day?"

Gwen's lips pursed together as she pondered the question. "Not every day. They would take it in turns, him and Mrs. Penny. They both worked a few hours while the other one had a bit of time off."

Faye tilted her head to one side. "So, not much going on out of the ordinary."

Put out by the lack of discovery so far, Gwen leaned back in her seat. "To tell you the truth, he was quite boring, really. On Thursdays, the only day he didn't work at the tearooms, he would wear an old brown cap and a set of binoculars that used to dangle around his neck."

"Oh," Faye sat upright, now more interested.

Gwen's eyes lit up, realizing she had Faye's attention.

"Oh well. Yes. Ten o'clock sharp every Thursday morning, he would meet Bill Green outside the teashop and head off."

"Where to?" Faye said, even more interested.

"To the woods, mostly."

"The woods?"

"Yes. He was a twitcher."

Faye stared bewildered at Gwen.

Gwen rolled her eyes.

"You know. He's one of those people who spend hours watching birds." She shrugged. "Heaven only knows why? Wilf would come in and tell us excitedly about some new bird or other he had discovered in the woods that hadn't been there before. But..." she added as she finished the last sip of her tea. "I wonder if he didn't just make up a lot of stories to impress Tina and me."

Faye put down her empty cup on the table. "Possibly. Do you know where the woods are? — Where he found those birds?"

Gwen shrugged again. "I never really listened half the time." She paused, "Come to think of it, he talked about this one 'special bird' he had discovered nesting. He said it was rare. But he would be secretive if you asked him any more about it."

"That is something worth telling Inspector Rawlings," Faye said, looking directly at her.

Gwen sat bolt upright, "You think I should tell Tom?"

Faye nodded, finishing the last bite of her biscuit.

"Yes! It may be a vital clue."

Gwen jumped up. "I'll go right now!"

Faye grabbed her coat, but Gwen had already rushed out through the bakery and was heading down the street towards the police station.

She stepped outside into the chill air, pulling her collar up around her neck and wondered if they had just discovered something of importance after all.

Chapter Three:
The Grand Opening

It was it was a rainy, dull, Thursday afternoon — not the sunny day that had been forecast. Faye peered through the teashop window and caught sight of Gwen and Tina running as fast as their legs would carry them across the road, trying to dodge puddles. Their arms were loaded with assorted trays of cakes and sandwiches covered in wax paper and white tea cloths. Daniel was sprinting down the street and met them at the door, holding it open as they all piled in.

Faye was distraught seeing them soaked to the skin.

"This is a disaster! How can we open today? And after all the hard work everyone from the village has put in!"

Daniel hung up his coat, still dripping on the floor. He grinned, a twinkle in his eye.

"Auntie Faye, don't be a wet blanket. It's because everyone pulled together that a bit of rain won't stop them from coming to the opening."

"We're all made of tougher stuff than that," Gwen chipped in, placing the wet tray down on the table.

Daniel clapped his hands and, rubbing them together, turned to Faye.

"Come on. Let's get to work."

He thrust one end of a string of alternating white, blue, and red fabric bunting into Faye's hand and started walking across to the front of the shop. He jumped onto a chair and reached up, looping one end of the string over a nail already placed in the tearoom wall.

"That's got it!" He said, stepping down off the chair.

Moving to the other side of the tearoom, Faye held out the bunting as he stepped up again, fixing it to the other wall. About an hour had passed before the four of them stood back to admire their handicraft. Wooden chairs sat neatly around small, round tables covered in white linen tablecloths. Tina had arranged a posy of sweet peas and pink roses gathered from the Station House garden and placed them into cream jugs in the center of the tables. Sat next to them were matching salt and pepper pots and rose-colored candles in mason jars.

Bunting adorned all four walls, and the teashop counter had now disappeared, groaning under the weight of trays burdened with sandwiches. Victorian sandwich cakes laden with whipped cream and jam, topped with fresh strawberries, made a spectacular display on the dresser next to them.

Faye fought back tears as she looked around at them.

"Thank you all so much."

"I couldn't have done it without all of you."

She had hardly finished speaking when the door to the tearoom flew open, and Inspector Rawlings came striding in, his coat flying up behind him. Water dripped from his hat as he reached up to take it off.

His eyes scanned the room, taking in the balloons and bunting strung out across the walls. His eyes finally settled on the trays of food across the counter.

"Very good," he said, bobbing up and down from his front feet to his heels excitedly at the sight of the enormous pile of cream cakes. "An impressive spread."

Secrets and Skeletons In The Teashop

Flustered, she took a china plate and handed it to him, looking away to avoid catching his eye.

"Thank you, inspector. Please help yourself."

Daniel looked over at the dessert-laden dresser, which now concealed the wall where Mr. Penny's skeleton had been discovered.

"And not a hint of Mr. Penny in sight!"

"Daniel!" Faye gasped. "Do you have to keep bringing that up?"

As the tearoom door opened again, Faye turned to see Margie walking in, followed by George Pennell. As she walked over to greet them, a steady flow of people from the village streamed in behind them. The rain had stopped, but no one noticed as laughter filled the room alongside the chinking of teacups and clatter of cutlery on plates. Gwen walked up to Faye, beaming a smile, and Faye detected a hint of excitement glance across her face.

"Faye, this is Mr. Green. Mr. Penny's friend."

She hesitated for a moment, trying to recall her conversation earlier that week with Gwen. Gwen nudged her arm, inclining her head towards him. "The twitcher."

Faye felt heat prickle her cheeks as he stared back at her. "Yes. Mr. Green. How lovely to meet you."

"Bill, please," he said, lifting his cap slightly to her. "Call me Bill." He glanced around the room. His eyes momentarily looked at the dresser before turning back to Faye. "It's a nice spread you've put on here."

"Thank you. But the credit goes to Gwen and Tina for all the time and effort they put into the baking today."

Gwen dismissed her statement with a flick of her hands. "Nonsense. It was teamwork. And anyway. I think it's always better when you have someone else to share the workload—or even a hobby with."

She turned sideways, blocking one side of her face from Bill's view, and winked at Faye. Faye coughed and reached for a glass of water, glaring wide-eyed at Gwen, who left them to bring out some more trays of sausage rolls. Left with an uncomfortable silence, Faye turned to Bill.

"I'm so sorry, Bill, about your friend, Mr. Penny."

Bill's expression turned vacant for a moment. "Thank you. He was a good friend." He nodded. "One of the best. Someone you could trust. Not like some..."

He was about to say something else when Lord Edmund Percy and his wife, Elizabeth, came over. Wearing a mink coat and bright red lipstick that set off her blue eyes, she looked every bit the Lady of the Manor as she kissed Faye on both cheeks.

"Wonderful opening, darling. Those little Mille Feuille slices are to die for. You must send me the recipe for my cook."

"Thank you, Elizabeth. I'll speak with Gwen. She has the recipe in a book from France."

Faye spun around to introduce Bill, but he had already moved back into the crowd.

....
....

It was four o'clock before the last guest left the teahouse. Daniel walked up to Faye, a wide grin stretched across his face.

Secrets and Skeletons In The Teashop

"Well, that was a resounding success! Congratulations, Auntie Faye. I think you've made your mark here in the village."

"Oh, definitely," Gwen added as they began clearing away.

"Did you get anywhere with Bill Green?"

"What's that?" Daniel asked as he overheard Gwen.

"Not really. He just said something about not trusting some people, but the Percys came up before I could ask him anything else."

Tina was pushing chairs under the tables at the front of the shop when she noticed the jacket hanging up by the front door.

"Is that yours, Daniel?" She asked, nodding to the jacket.

"It's not mine." He said, walking over. Someone has left it here.

Daniel dipped his hand into each pocket of the jacket, searching until he came out with a small notebook with an image of a bird on the cover. He flicked through the pages.

"It's Mr. Greens!" He announced, holding up the cover to show Faye. "His name is on the inside."

She walked over. "I think we should just put the notebook back in his jacket. He'll probably come looking for it when he realizes he left it here. Just as Daniel shut the notebook, Faye reached out and stopped him from closing the page with her hand. The letters "B. E.G" stood out, scribbled in bold across the page.

"On second thought." She grasped it from his hands. "I'll just hang onto it for safekeeping."

Daniel raised an eyebrow and stared at Faye.

"I know that look, Auntie Faye. Is something afoot?"

She slid the book into her apron pocket. "I'm not sure yet."

Later that evening, Faye sat in her favorite wingback chair by the fire with Buster at her feet and thumbed through the notebook.

"Well, Buster," she mused, flicking backwards and forwards through the pages. "There are a few names in here, but still not much to go on." She snapped the book shut, making Buster sit up. Leaving the book on the arm of the chair she made her way upstairs with Buster following close behind.

"Tomorrow, Buster, we are going to pay a visit to Mr. Green."

Secrets and Skeletons In The Teashop

Chapter Four:
Bill Green

It was six o'clock in the morning when Buster woke Faye, pulling at the bedcovers.

"It's too early to get up," Faye moaned at Buster, turning over. But he kept pulling at the covers until she gave in and sat up.

"Okay. Okay. You win." Putting her dressing gown on, she walked down the stairs and heard someone lightly knocking on the kitchen door. Cautiously opening the door, she recognized the small stout figure of Bill Green, binoculars dangling around his neck.

"Sorry to knock so early, Miss Lantern—Faye," he said, tipping his cap as she peered around the door at him. "But I think I left my jacket here yesterday."

"Yes. Of course. I was going to return it to you today. Please come in. I'll get it for you."

She opened the door, and he stepped in after her.

"Would you like some tea? I was just about to put the kettle on."

"Not for me. Thank you." He tapped his hand on the battered leather satchel hanging down from his shoulder. "I have a flask ready to go." Faye nodded, hurried into the tearooms, and returned with his jacket.

"That's grand Faye. You said you were going to return it to me. How did you know it was mine?"

Faye's cheeks flushed as she replied,

"Oh. It was your notebook." And realizing she had left it on her chair last night, rushed into the dining room to pick it up.

"There you are," she said, quickly handing it to him as she walked back into the kitchen. "We looked through the pockets to get some clues about the owner. I hope you don't mind."

"Normally, I would." He said, taking the notebook from her. "If it fell into the wrong hands." His voice trailed off.

Intrigued, she said. "The wrong hands?"

Bill's voice lowered to a whisper as he leaned in. "There are some folks who would pay a handsome price for what's written in here." He tapped the notebook on his nose and nodded his head as he spoke.

"Really?" Faye said, interested in him to continue. He leaned in again.

"Me and Wilf — Mr. Penny, we were the only two people who knew where the Eagles were nesting. It's all in here." He tapped his notebook again with his finger.

"You have the location of the Eagles' secret nesting sites in there? Isn't that a risk if someone discovered your notebook?"

The corners of his mouth creased back into a smile. "Ah. But you wouldn't know where....." he exaggerated. "It's in code."

Faye's eyes lit up as Bill opened the notebook.

"See here," he pointed to the letters.

"B. is Badgers Wood. E. is Emery Down. And G," he stopped. "Well. That's still a secret, mind you."

Secrets and Skeletons In The Teashop

Faye could hear Daniel's approaching footsteps from his apartment, making his way down the stairs as Bill snapped the notebook shut.

"Thank you for my jacket, Faye." He lifted his arm, holding the jacket.

"I won't keep you any longer." Tipping his cap, he left abruptly, leaving Faye standing there as Daniel reached the bottom of the stairs.

Yawning, Daniel made his way to the fridge. "Did I hear voices?"

"Yes. It was Mr. Green, come to collect his jacket." She sighed. Disappointed at not being able to question him any further.

"So early?" he said, peering into the fridge with one hand on the open door.

"I think he was heading off to go birdwatching. Apparently, there is some secret around where the birds are nesting."

"They must be rare birds then," he said, triumphantly finding the bacon and turning it around with the plate. "Mostly, they keep the location a secret so that people don't steal the eggs from their nests."

Faye frowned. "Those poor birds. Why would anyone want to steal their eggs?"

With a frying pan in one hand, Daniel lifted the bacon slices and dropped them in one by one. "Because they can be worth a lot of money to collectors. It depends on the birds, of course. But the rarer the bird, the more money the eggs fetch."

She moved around the kitchen counter, closing the fridge door as he said, "It's all illegal, mind you. But it's big business. The poachers get paid a small fortune for the eggs if they are in good condition."

Falling quiet, she pondered what Daniel had said, wondering if Mr. Penny's death was connected to it all, either as an innocent victim or an accomplice.

Deep in thought, she walked off into the hallway to get Buster's lead. Buster was sitting, dribbling at Daniel's feet, reluctant to leave. Entering the kitchen again, she reached down, put Buster's collar on, and tugged him away. "I'm going to walk Buster down to the station." Her mind now on Inspector Rawlings — her heart quickened at the thought of seeing him again.

"Right you are," Daniel called back, gingerly dropping a burnt piece of toast onto his plate.

Chapter Five:
A Rare Bird

Faye left with a brisk walk down to the station. Inspector Rawlings was sitting behind his desk as Constable Pemberley showed her through. His blonde, unruly hair gave him a boyish charm, and he greeted her with a huge welcoming smile, jumping up from his chair.

"Miss Lantern. Please come in. Take a seat."

He looked over to Buster and patted him on the head, happy they had worked out an agreement as he broke a piece of his sandwich from his desk drawer and gave it to him.

Faye pulled out the chair and sat down.

"Thank you, Inspector. I wanted to talk with you about Mr. Green."

"Bill Green?" He asked, sitting back down.

"Yes. He had a notebook just like Mr. Penny's, and I've discovered what those letters mean."

"I'm ahead of you there, Miss Lantern. These are the bird-watching sites they visited."

Surprised and disappointed at the same time that he already knew, she clasped her hands together awkwardly and mumbled, "Oh. Well then. That's good."

He nodded. "I brought him in for questioning again. He was a prime suspect at the time and still not in the clear."

Faye couldn't hide the surprise in her voice. "Surely you can't think Bill had anything to do with Mr. Penny's murder?" She paused, searching his eyes for a response. "Do you?"

"We can't rule him out as a suspect yet. He was the last person to see Wilfred Penny alive."

Faye leaned back in her seat. It didn't sit well with her. "But what would be his motive? He seemed positive that Mr. Penny was a dear and trusted friend."

She watched him gather the scattered papers together on his desk and put them in a pile that looked as unruly as his hair.

"It seems they had a falling out the night of Wilfred's murder. Wilfred wanted to check on the falcon's nest, and after an argument, Bill said he walked home and left Wilfred on his own, making his way to the nesting site."

"Did he tell you where the nesting site was?"

"Yes. The old quarry pit at 'Grimmers Point.'" He stopped and stared at her, "This is confidential information, Miss Lantern, and I'll ask you to treat it as such."

"Of course, inspector. But that still doesn't give Bill a motive to murder his friend?"

There was a brief knock on the office door.

"Come in."

Constable Pemberley took a step in. "Excuse me, inspector, but I have someone ready in room three."

"Thank you, Pemberley." He turned back to Faye. "If you don't mind, Miss Lantern, I have an interview to conduct."

Secrets and Skeletons In The Teashop

Faye sprung up from her chair. "Of course."

He stood up and held eye contact with her, a warmth in his voice as he said, "I appreciate you coming by."

Her cheeks flushed as she smiled and acknowledged him. Quickly picking up Buster's lead, she headed to the door.

"Good day, Inspector…Come on, Buster. I have a meeting with someone, too."

Chapter Six:
Mrs. Penny

Mrs. Penny had been quite a looker in her day — Faye had been told by several people in the village, winning the beauty pageant for several years. With her frail body now hunched over in the wheelchair, it was hard to recognize the beauty queen she once was. She cleared her throat, alerting Mrs. Penny, who looked up from her chair, her face gaunt and expressionless, staring silently at Faye.

"Hello, Mrs. Penny. I'm Faye Lantern. I've just moved into the Station House."

She seemed startled at the mention of the Station House, her fingers gripping tighter on the arm of her wheelchair.

"I just wanted to pop in and tell you that the Station House is in good hands, and I've just reopened the tearooms."

The sunlight coming through the window caught Mrs. Penny's face as tears filled her eyes. She turned her head away, and Faye's stomach lurched, wondering if she had taken too much of a liberty, visiting her under false pretenses. Did Mrs. Penny even know that it was her husband's dead body in the tearoom walls? This was a terrible mistake on her part.

"Maybe I'll come back to visit another day." She wasn't able to finish the sentence as Mrs. Penny raised her hand.

"One moment, please."

She turned and gazed at Faye, her cheeks glistening with tears. Clutching a white handkerchief, she dabbed around them.

Secrets and Skeletons In The Teashop

"Forgive me. Where are my manners? I'm Jane. It's wonderful to meet you. Won't you take a seat?"

Too late to make her excuses, she walked over to the armchair opposite Mrs. Penny and sat down. A dark wood cabinet glanced the ceiling towering over them from across the room. Brightly colored china teapots, cups, and saucers in hues of pinks, blues, and green dotted with flowers adorned every shelf. A rose teapot stood center stage, probably a vestige of the Station House tearooms and a treasured memento.

"That was the tea set we were using when Wilfred proposed to me," she said, noticing Faye's attention on the teapot. "It was my mother's. First given to her as a wedding present from her mother, and she passed it down to us on our wedding day."

She dabbed at her eyes with her handkerchief again.

"Those were the happiest days of my life when Wilfred and I first moved into the station house after we were married. A look of happiness glanced across her face as she stared at Faye. I'm glad you have reopened it again."

Faye smiled. "I couldn't have done it without the help of the villagers. They have been so kind and given so much of their time to come and help me. The renovations were…."

She paused as the vision of Mr. Penny's skeleton in the walls came flooding back.

"Um. Well. Err." Her mind searching for something else to say as Mrs. Penny interrupted.

"It's okay. I know about Wilfred's body."

Faye sighed. Relieved she hadn't put her foot in it.

"Inspector Rawlings visited me yesterday. He told me about how you found…" she stopped, catching her breath before bursting into deep, heart-wrenching sobs — clutching her handkerchief to her mouth. Whenever Faye had been in this situation before, there were always eager people — women usually — who would rush forward to comfort the person who was upset, which had suited Faye perfectly well up to this point. She stared at Mrs. Penny, aware no one was rushing to her aid, as she sobbed into her handkerchief. Anxiety crept over her as, reluctantly, she stood up. Deprived of the warmth and security of her mother's embrace as she grew up, she felt ill-prepared to give comfort, but she cared and, seeing Mrs. Penny so distraught, walked over and placed a hand on her shoulder.

"I'm so sorry for your loss. It must have been a terrible shock."

Mrs. Penny's shoulders heaved as she sobbed again. Faye stood with her in silence, her hand resting on her shoulder until her cries of pain slowed down, and she could breathe again.

She reached up for Faye's hand on her shoulder, patting it, then lowered her hand, twisting the handkerchief she was clutching, turning it over and over.

"Love has so many faces."

Faye's hand fell away, trying to work out what she meant as Mrs. Penny tugged at the bottom of her shawl, straightening it up.

"Do you have any family, Faye? Any children?"

Faye wandered over to the large window, streaming sunlight into the room. Breathtaking views over the harbor and out to sea greeted her. Spellbound, she watched the boats in the harbor bob up and down on the water for a few seconds before replying.

"I have my nephew, Daniel. He's staying with me at the Station House. He is a great comfort to me. But no children as of yet."

Secrets and Skeletons In The Teashop

Mrs. Penny pushed at a stray grey hair that had fallen on her face.

"I always wanted a daughter. I would have liked to have passed on my mother's tea set." She sighed. A silent despair etched into every line on her face. "My son isn't interested in that kind of thing."

Faye walked back to the chair and sat down. With an upbeat tone in her voice, she replied, "Maybe he might change his mind one day?"

Mrs. Penny shook her head. "Terrance never cared about the tearoom, and I don't think he will be interested in my mother's teapot unless it's...." She turned to Faye, her face strained. "He hasn't visited me for several years, and perhaps it's for the best." She turned away. "Sometimes things are better left in the past."

Faye didn't want to upset her any more than she already had. But she had an inkling she was hiding something. "What do you mean?"

Mrs. Penny's eyes hardened as she stared back at her. "Nothing is going to bring back, Wilfred. I don't think dragging up the past will serve any purpose."

"But surely you want to find who is…" Faye stopped, searching for the right words. "Who is guilty of taking Wilfred's life?"

Mrs. Penny shook her head. "It doesn't matter now. If you don't mind, Faye, I would like to rest."

Slightly put out that instead of finding answers, the mystery around Wilfred's death had now deepened, Faye stood up. "Of course. I am sorry to have kept you for so long. It can't have been easy for you to recall such painful memories."

Mrs. Penny didn't reply. She sat silently, staring out the window as Faye tried to get her attention again.

Penny Townsend

"Well. It was lovely to meet you in person. Perhaps I could pop in again – to let you know how the tearoom is doing."

She wasn't sure if Mrs. Penny could see through her ruse of being desperate to find out what she was hiding, but she comforted herself that visiting her would be a welcome break for her in an otherwise lonely existence. Relieved to see her head nod in acknowledgment, she walked out the door, and Mrs. Penny sat alone in her sadness, with secrets that weighed heavily upon her.

Chapter Seven:
The Invitation

It had been two days since Faye had spoken with Jane Penny. On her way back from the post office, she was still mulling over the details as she arrived back home. Going through the Station House door, she stepped back just in time to catch Buster's collar as he ran towards her, nearly knocking her over.

"Sorry!" Daniel shouted. "We are just on our way out."

Buster ran back and jumped up, trying to grab the lead from Daniel's hand in excitement.

"Siii…t" he said, dragging out the word, to which Buster promptly plonked down, his tail wagging furiously.

Faye's face lit up. "Oh, well done!"

Daniel handed him a biscuit as a reward, and a second later, Buster jumped up again, much to his despair.

He sighed, "It's a work in progress."

Faye stifled a laugh. It was such a joy having Daniel and Buster at the Station House.

"I'm making beef stew and dumplings for tea, as a treat, if you would like some?"

Daniel turned his head as he walked down the hallway. "Great! I'll look forward to that. Beef stew. One of my favorites!"

Her heart leaped as she glimpsed Inspector Rawlings in the doorway. He quickly removed his hat before patting Buster.

Daniel nodded to him, "Inspector." Then, he set off at a brisk pace with Buster down to the canal for some more training.

Faye could feel her cheeks flush as she smiled. "Please come in, Inspector. I'm just about to make a pot of tea."

A few minutes later, she set down the tea tray in the dining room to see him studying the chessboard on the table. Their game had been going on for a few weeks, and Faye relished the opportunity to play as he picked up a black rook and moved it across the board.

"I hear you visited Mrs. Penny a few days ago at the nursing home," he said, looking up.

A pang of guilt made her turn away.

"How did you know that?"

"I had a telephone call from her son, complaining that you had distressed his mother."

Faye frowned, remembering how much Mrs. Penny had cried whilst she was there.

"I'm so sorry. That wasn't my intention at all."

He walked over to the small table that she had put the tray of sandwiches on.

"He's usually the one upsetting people. I take what he says with a pinch of salt."

She pursed her lips as she remembered her visit with Mrs. Penny, "I think she was hiding something."

Without looking up, he continued loading his plate with sandwiches, "Really. Like what?"

Secrets and Skeletons In The Teashop

"I'm not sure. But she said Mr. Penny's murder should be left in the past?"

A flash of determination crossed his eyes, his brow furrowed as he turned to her.

"I have a duty to investigate if I suspect a crime has been committed! Anyway. It's out of Mrs. Penny's hands now."

Faye took a sip of her tea and nodded, looking away. She wasn't used to his steely tone.

"Do you know much about her son?"

"Terrance Penny?" he said, about to bite into a sandwich.

"If my memory serves me, he got caught fencing stolen jewelry and spent a few years in prison."

Wide-eyed, Faye put her cup down as he walked over and sat down opposite her.

"It happened after the Penny's threw him out. He used to demand money from them and became violent with old man Penny when he refused to give him anymore. I was glad he telephoned, actually. I've asked him in for questioning."

"About his father's murder?"

"Yes. He was still living in the village at the time of Mr. Penny's disappearance. I've checked the records, and he said he was rock climbing with his best friend, who had the same story and a very convenient alibi for him."

She lifted the teapot and poured out the tea.

"Doesn't that put him in the clear, then?" Her heart wanted to find reasons to avoid the thought that Terrance had killed his own father.

He shook his head. "No. There's some confusion as to where they were climbing. Someone saw his car parked at Grimmer Point, but that conflicts with his story that they parked at Deer Leap Way, which is a mile down the road."

"Grimmer Point? Isn't that where the eagles are nesting?"

"Yes. It was right on top of the nesting sight and the last place Mr. Penny had visited, if we can believe Bill Green's version of events. So, I'm bringing him in for questioning again."

"What about his friend?"

"He died in a motorcycle accident last year. So, we only have Terrance's story to go on now."

She watched him juggle the plate and his tea, his hair falling into blonde waves around his face.

"Do you think you'll discover any additional evidence after all this time?"

"I believe persistence and dogged determination to get to the truth is all you need to bring any fresh evidence to light."

She relaxed back in her chair. The few years of time that had elapsed since Mr. Penny's death had not deterred him in the slightest from trying to get to the truth and solve the case.

"Maybe now you have the body…bones of Mr. Penny. You may have some fresh evidence?"

"That's a possibility. I'll know more when we get forensics back." He stood up.

His face softened. "Well, as always, it was a pleasure, but I have a mountain of paperwork calling."

He hesitated, standing uneasily in front of her, and she noticed a bead of sweat gather on his brow.

"I'm going over to Grimmers Point tomorrow to get a better idea of the layout around the nesting site before I interview Terrance Penny."

His eyes focused on her with an intensity that made her feel unnerved and alive at the same time.

"Maybe you would like to accompany me? You have an eye for detail, and I could use an extra pair of hands."

Uncertain if it was normal to be asked to go on police business, she pushed the thought from her mind as, frankly, she didn't care. Her heart raced in anticipation of spending time with him.

"I'd be delighted."

He blinked, staring at her as if surprised. Suddenly coming to his senses, he straightened up.

"Good. Well, then. I'll pick you up at seven o'clock sharp tomorrow morning." He nodded at her and hurried out the door.

Chapter Eight:
Grimmer Point

The mist rolling in engulfed the cliffs as Faye and Inspector Rawlings stepped out of the car at Grimmer Point. Buster took off at a run, sniffing the ground as they both stood at the bottom of the cliff, looking up.

The sun had broken through the clouds and glanced down on the winding trail to where they stood. Inspector Rawlings inclined his head up towards the cliff.

"I'll head up and get a better view of the area."

The steep cliff face towered above them, and Faye was glad he offered to go alone. Her gaze turned towards the two cliffs that abutted each other, their peeks barely visible in the mist.

"I'll follow the path through the cliffs further down this way."

The inspector strode off up the trail as she made her way around the base, treading slowly and carefully, now and then steadying herself against the rock with her hand. After about forty minutes, the shrill of a bird calling made her crane her neck up towards the sky. An eagle wheeled between the clouds and the vastness of the blue sky and called out again, joined by its mate. They soared in circles, gliding and swooping in a freefall dance before they moved off into the distance.

She smiled at the freedom they exhibited, her mind cast back to the day she promised Tommy she would wait for him. The myriad of changes in her life now left her feeling unsettled. Tired, she looked around for somewhere to sit when she heard footsteps behind her. A tall, clean-shaven man in his early thirties, wearing a black leather jacket and trousers, was standing there. His eyes deep set and sunken in, he stood, one boot on the ground, the other raised,

Secrets and Skeletons In The Teashop

balancing on a rock. He drew on a cigarette, studying Faye as he blew smoke from his slightly parted lips, now blocking her exit on the narrow path. Buster made a low rumbling sound, and she reached down with her hand to reassure him, glad of his presence.

"It's okay, Buster."

She heard Inspector Rawling's voice calling her in the distance, and relief flooded her as she went to call out but stopped, immobilized by the man's eyes now narrowed and focused on her, daring her to call out. Her heart beat faster when he suddenly turned and disappeared back the way he came. Before she could catch her breath, Inspector Rawlings appeared.

"There you are!" he said, relief in his voice. "I was getting worried when I didn't hear from you."

He stopped. Noticing her ashen face. "Has something happened? You look like you've seen a ghost!"

"Not a ghost. But a man appeared right where you are standing." She pointed towards the path behind him. "Then he disappeared the same way."

The inspector looked back around.

"You must have passed him on the path?"

"No," he said confidently. "No one came past me. I am certain of that."

Puzzled, Faye frowned. "That's not possible!"

She rushed past him to where the man had disappeared and looked along the cliff. Her eyes searching along the wall, she crouched down, her hands tracing a well-worn curve on the rock wall that jutted out from the cliff.

"Over here!" she called out and disappeared behind the rock. She could hear the inspector scrambling down the path behind her as she emerged into an enormous dome-shaped cave. Light flooded in from an opening on the other wall, which led down and around the Cliff.

"He must have left this way." She followed another trail to the outside, which wound around the side of the cliff face.

Inspector Rawlings glanced at the opening. "Someone could easily get away unnoticed here."

He stepped back and turned to Faye. "Did he say who he was?"

Faye shook her head, "He didn't speak at all. He wasn't there long enough."

Her eye caught sight of a small wooden box on the cave floor, a glint of sunlight just catching its open lid. Inspector Rawlings was already striding over to investigate it and bent down.

"This looks like a box for transporting birds' eggs."

Faye remembered her conversation with Daniel. "For stealing eagle eggs, maybe?"

"Judging by the size of the compartments, I'd say so." He straightened up.

"I'll take this back to the station and check it out properly."

They walked back out of the cave, and it was a relief to feel the sunlight on her face again. As they reached the end of the path, Buster caught the scent of a rabbit and rushed off, nose to the ground.

"Buster, come back!"

Secrets and Skeletons In The Teashop

Faye called in vain. She waited by the car for him to finish sniffing around the burrow hole which the rabbit had long since disappeared down, as Inspector Rawlings stood next to her.

"Well, Miss Lantern. That was a fruitful expedition. I knew it was the right thing to ask you along. We should do this more often."

Faye's cheeks flushed as he smiled at her; his ruffled hair moved in the breeze in unruly opposition to his disciplined nature, and, for the first time in a long time, her heart stirred.

Buster came bowling over, interrupting her thoughts as he bumped into her legs, knocking her off balance. The inspector caught her arm, and their eyes locked in an intense gaze as he held her. For a moment, she longed to stay alone with him.

"Thank you, Inspector." She said and pulled her arm away to open the car door. The last time she looked at Thomas before he left for war, she had felt the same way.

Chapter Nine:
Hidden In Plain Sight

Inspector Rawlings looked carefully at the wooden box, turning it around in his hands. Loose straw spilled out over his desk. He picked up a single yellow strand and twisted it in his fingers.

"This is more serious than we thought, Pemberley. This straw is fresh."

The young police constable stared at the box. "You think the box is being used now?"

"Yes," he said, carefully pushing the loose strands back into one of the compartments.

"I would hazard a guess we still have active poachers stealing birds' eggs in the area. I think we may have disturbed them this morning."

His hand reached for the telephone on his desk, and, picking up the receiver, he dialed the Old Station House. Hearing Faye's voice, he coughed nervously.

"Erm. Yes, Miss Lantern. It's Inspector Rawlings."

Faye's mind instantly drifted back to the moment their eyes met at the car as he spoke.

"Could you stop by the station to describe the man you met in the cave this morning?"

"Yes, of course." A slight disappointment in her voice. Part of her was hoping he wanted her to accompany him again.

"Would tomorrow be okay?"

Secrets and Skeletons In The Teashop

"Yes. I'll tell the desk sergeant to keep an eye out for you. Thank you, Miss Lantern." He abruptly ended the call.

Faye placed the receiver back down. She had a lot of work ahead of her today, getting the tea rooms ready for the large group of cyclists who had already booked their end-of-race refreshments. She would have to go to the police station early to fit it all in.

The first cyclist caught Faye's eye, hurtling by the tearoom window, followed by several others. One after the other, heads down, legs peddling faster than train wheels turning to reach the finish line. As the tearoom door opened, she heard the cheers and applause coming from outside grow louder.

"You should have seen the winner, Faye! He had legs of steel!"

Gwen was about to go into a more detailed description when the door opened again, and Bill Green walked in.

"Hello, Faye, Gwen," he said, tipping his cap at them.

"Could I please have a pot of tea and an assortment of your fresh scones with extra cream and jam?"

His order caught Gwen's attention. "Ooh. Are you celebrating something, Bill?"

He sat down casually at the small corner table. "Only what a beautiful day it is."

He looked away from her and out the window. Gwen's disbelieving look didn't go unnoticed by Faye as she placed the scones on a plate.

"Can you pass me another pot of jam, please, Gwen?"

She picked up the jam and handed it to Faye.

"He's up to something!" she said in a whisper, filling up the teapot with hot water.

Faye sighed. "I'm sure that's not the case."

Gwen curled her top lip up in disdain. Still not giving up on her theory, she reached across, taking a tray from the already prepared stack, and added.

"I have a nose for these things. He's probably meeting a lover." She winked.

"Well, what if he is? It's none of our business," she snapped.

Gwen raised an eyebrow as Faye looked over at her. Embarrassed and wanting to forget her curt reply, she busied herself, filling the cream jugs and putting them next to the jam.

"Can you take the tray over to Bill and please," she emphasized, "let him enjoy the scones in peace."

Gwen picked up the tray and, with a glint in her eye, turned on her heel.

"Okay. But I'm going to keep my eye on him."

Faye despaired at Gwen, always wanting to know everyone's business. Sometimes, she thought she took it too far. Now, her feelings towards Inspector Rawlings were making her act out of sorts, and imagining Gwen would pick up on it was too difficult for her to deal with right now.

Daniel burst through the tearoom door, making her jump.

"They're on the way, Aunty Faye!"

Secrets and Skeletons In The Teashop

A gaggle of excited voices followed as the cyclists flooded in behind him, keeping Faye and Gwen rushed off their feet.

"I thought you said there would only be ten of them?" Gwen said as she took the eighth tray of sandwiches, tea, and cakes to a group of three of the last weary cyclists that had just joined the group.

"There's at least twenty-five, by my reckoning. Not to mention Bill and his friend as well."

Faye looked over to where Bill was sitting, unable to see through the group standing in the middle, greeting each other.

"I wasn't expecting so many of them," she said as Gwen disappeared again.

By late afternoon, the last of the cyclists had left the tearoom, and Faye stood, hands on hips, gazing around the room at the sea of empty cups and plates strewn across every table. Gwen walked over, a tea towel draped over her arm. She blew a curl off her face.

"Well! That was a fine to do!"

The tearoom door opened behind Faye, making her turn around.

"Have I missed out on the cakes?"

"Inspector!" Her cheeks flushed at the sight of him smiling at her.

"Of course not. There are a few cakes and sandwiches still left over out the back. I'll get them for you."

Glad to be out of his presence so she could recompose herself, she rushed off.

Gwen smiled as he stood at the counter.

Penny Townsend

"Great timing, as usual, Tom!"

Faye came back with a plate full of food and looked around for a space to lay the tray down. Gwen was already walking towards the corner table with an empty tray in her hand.

"This one is the least messy — Except for these loose bits of straw."

She put the tray down and started brushing the straw off the table with her hand.

"This was where Bill was sitting! He was with that odd-looking biker. But I can't see why there would be straw on the table, though?"

Faye looked over and rolled her eyes. "There were a lot of bikers in here today, Gwen."

"Not that type. I meant a motorbike type. He was the moody sort, but he kind of looked familiar. He was wearing black leather and boots."

Faye froze. An image of the man in the cave sprung to her mind. Inspector Rawlings walked over to where Gwen was standing. He picked up a single piece of loose straw from the table missed by Gwen and rolled it between his fingers.

"Are you talking about Bill Green, Mr. Penny's twitcher friend?"

"Yes. He was with the biker."

Faye placed the pile of plates she was holding down on the countertop, steadied herself, took a deep breath, and relaxed again. Grabbing a handful of sandwiches, Inspector Rawlings strode back over to Faye and tipped his hat to her.

Secrets and Skeletons In The Teashop

"Thank you for the sandwiches. I can't stay." A look passed between them, making her realize her heart was fighting a losing battle. He hesitated, then turned on his heel and rushed out the tearoom door.

Gwen turned to Faye. "What was all that about? "

Faye watched him through the shop window, rushing down the street.

"I suspect he wants to question Bill about birds' eggs and — Mr. Penny's death."

Chapter Ten:
The Letter

Faye relaxed back in her favorite armchair. Taking a sip of tea, she heard a thud on the front door mat. Puzzled, as the mail had already been delivered, she went into the hall. A brown envelope with Faye's name and address at the Station House sat on the mat. Buster ran up and sniffed the envelope. He made a low grumble and barked.

"What is it, Buster?" she asked, picking up the envelope and opening it as she walked into the kitchen to read the hand-written letter.

Dear Faye,

After your visit the other day, a past wound has opened in me and I can't live with myself if I don't tell someone before I leave this earth. My Wilf wasn't a perfect man, but I loved him, and he didn't deserve what happened to him. That's why I'm writing this letter, to tell you the truth. God, forgive me, but I helped put Wilf's dead body in the walls of the tearoom. I've tortured myself ever since. Nothing will bring him back, I know, and I don't expect you or anyone else to understand, but I did it to protect my son, who is innocent.

Please tell Inspector Rawlings that Wilf's death is better left in the past.

Thank you for your visit. You seem like a kind soul, and I'm glad the tea shop is in your hands.

Yours Faithfully,

Jane Penny.

Secrets and Skeletons In The Teashop

Faye pulled the kitchen chair out and sat down in shock to re-read the letter. Part of her empathized with Mrs. Penny. She couldn't imagine how awful it must have been to have suffered, holding on to a secret like that all those years. But she didn't say if she knew who murdered Wilfred. The only obvious thing was she was still trying to protect Terrance.

She put the letter on the table, walked into the hallway, and called the police station. They passed her through to the inspector, who was quick to answer.

"Miss Lantern. How may I be of help?"

"Hello Inspector. I have a rather interesting letter from Jane Penny that I think you will want to read."

She took a breath in before adding, "She has confessed to putting her husband's body in the tearoom walls."

There was a moment of silence before he said, "I'll be right over." And hung up.

Inspector Rawlings looked tense as he walked in the door. He had a habit of gritting his teeth when he was under pressure, and his face was strained. She missed his warm smile as she handed him the letter.

He spoke formally after reading the letter. "When did you receive this, Miss Lantern?"

"It was only a short while ago. Not much before I called you."

His eyes cast to the corner of the envelope. "There's no stamp."

"I noticed that too. It was hand-delivered, but I don't know who put it through the letterbox."

He tucked the letter in his coat pocket. "I didn't realize you knew Mrs. Penny that well."

Faye blushed. "I only popped in to visit her as I took over the tea shop," she added quickly. "That was the visit Terrance complained about."

He nodded. "Did she reveal anything about Mr. Penny's death, then?"

"No. She didn't. But she seemed upset when she talked about Terrance."

"Well, something has made her send this to you." His face was now concerned.

"I want you to be careful, Miss Lantern. It seems to me Mrs. Penny knows more than she is telling us."

He tucked the letter inside his jacket pocket. "Until we have more evidence to go on, please be vigilant, and do not," he stressed, "pay any more visits to Mrs. Penny until I have sorted this business out."

He stared long enough at her that her heart started beating faster. She looked away.

"Of course."

Daniel whistled, sauntering down the hallway as Inspector Rawlings rushed past him and out the door. He stopped to watch the inspector disappear and turned back to Faye.

"What's going on?"

"I'm sad to say I had a letter from Mrs. Penny saying she helped put Wilfred's dead body in the teashop walls."

Secrets and Skeletons In The Teashop

Daniel, open-mouthed, stared at Faye as she continued,

"She made it sound like it wasn't her or Terrance that killed him. And she's asked Inspector Rawlings not to investigate any further as she says her son is innocent."

She inclined her head.

"Which has lit a fire under him to get to the truth of what happened."

Still in shock, Daniel rested his hands on his hip.

"Well! It seems Mr. Penny isn't dying quietly even after all these years!"

He thought for a moment.

"If Mrs. Penny hasn't admitted to killing Wilf and her son is innocent... If we believe her, then..."

He looked at Faye as the realization dawned on them both. The actual killer could be in the village right now, and nobody knew who they were.

Chapter Eleven:
Terrance

Inspector Rawlings stood with his hat in hand, talking with one of the care home nurses. He scratched his head in frustration before thanking the nurse and strode out of the care home, slamming the car door shut after him. Back at the station, Constable Pemberley was escorting Terrance Penny in handcuffs along the corridor. He shoved a struggling Terrance into the interview room and onto the chair as he walked in.

"Thank you, Pemberley. I'll take it from here."

He sat down opposite Terrance, who scowled angrily at him.

"You've got no right bringing me in. I haven't done nothin'!" He held Inspector Rawling's gaze.

"I'm afraid I have some bad news for you, Terrance. Your mother passed away a few hours ago."

A look of disbelief and shock clung to Terrance's face. His eyes stared blankly at Inspector Rawlings, who stared back, unwavering, confirming to Terrance the truth of his mother's passing. He dropped his head in silence and looked away, reaching down and patting his pocket, looking for his cigarettes. He pulled the box out awkwardly between his cuffed hands. Inspector Rawlings got up and spoke to Constable Pemberley outside, who came back with a silver lighter, holding the flame in front of Terrance to light his cigarette, and then left the room. Inspector Rawlings sat down again. His manner was now softer.

"I'm sorry for your loss, Terrance."

Terrance drew on his cigarette and glanced towards him. "We weren't that close…. She changed after Dad…."

Secrets and Skeletons In The Teashop

He looked away again as wisps of cigarette smoke curled around his lips.

"Do you know what happened to your father?"

He shrugged and leaned back slightly in his chair.

"He wasn't the perfect man most people thought he was."

Inspector Rawlings fixed his gaze on him. "What do you mean?"

Terrance shifted uncomfortably in his chair. "I mean, the old man had a devil of a temper and wasn't afraid to use his fists."

Inspector Rawlings fell silent - memories of his own father's beatings still haunting him. "Are you saying he beat you?"

Terrance's lips clenched tightly around the cigarette in his mouth. His cuffed hands reached up, taking it. His head leaned backward as he blew a stream of smoke upwards.

"Yeah. And not just me. He beat my mother so hard one day he knocked her out."

Inspector Rawlings saw his opportunity. "So, you took your revenge on him?"

Terrance's eyes narrowed in defiance and his fists clenched. "I left when I was eighteen. I never saw him again."

He wanted to keep the pressure on. It was a risk. Terrance could explode in a rage at any moment, ruining his chance of finding out the truth. But he needed answers.

"So how did he end up being bricked up in the tea shop walls? Did your mother kill him?"

His nostrils flared in anger as he turned his face away to avoid eye contact.

"My mother wouldn't hurt no one. I told her to leave him years ago, but she wouldn't."

He leaned forward. "Do you know who killed your father?"

A small hesitancy before his reply told him all he needed to know.

"No!"

He lowered his voice, easing the pressure. "I know your mother helped put your father in the Tearoom walls."

Terrance's eyes looked frightened for the first time since he had entered the interview room. He quickly spun away and stubbed his cigarette in the ashtray.

"Can you tell me anything about your father's murder, Terrance?"

"Nope!"

Inspector Rawlings slumped back. He needed more evidence before he made any arrests. Experience told him Terrance would not tell him anything more today. If he was involved in the smuggling of the eagles' eggs, as he suspected, then he wanted to find out who his contacts were.

"You're free to go."

Terrance looked up in surprise as he called in Constable Pemberley.

"Drive Terrance back home — and get his passport."

Secrets and Skeletons In The Teashop

As Inspector Rawlings went to leave, Terrance grabbed his arm, stopping him in his tracks. "No good will come of poking around now. Leave this in the past, for everyone's sake."

Inspector Rawling's eyes hardened as he looked down at Terrance and pulled his arm away, "I think your murdered father would see it differently," and walked out the door.

Chapter Twelve:
A Disturbing Turn of Events

Inspector Rawlings threw the file onto his desk. Cold cases were difficult to gather good evidence on. As he was leaving, the telephone rang, and he spun around and picked up the receiver.

"Thank you," he replied, replacing the receiver. He shook his head and walked out of his office.

....
....

A flurry of nurses rushed around the care home as Inspector Rawlings walked in. The tension was palpable, as every now and again, nurses would huddle together in a group and whisper and then move off again in a hurry. The staff nurse greeted Inspector Rawlings with a half-hearted smile.

"Good morning, Inspector. I'm Staff Nurse Botley."

The morning had been wearing on her, and her usual neatly tied-back hair had fallen out of place, matching her fraught demeanor.

"Of all the years I've worked here, Inspector, nothing like this has ever taken place!" Pulling open the desk drawer, she grabbed a key.

"I expect you want to see her room?"

He nodded. "Yes. We can start there."

She opened the office door and marched down the corridor, stopping at Mrs. Penny's old room. Unlocking the door, she threw it open. Walking in with the inspector following, she declared, "No one has touched anything here since Mrs. Penny's death," She shook her head. "Who would do such a thing to a poor old lady?"

"That's what I'm about to find out." He looked around the room. "Can you get me a list of all her visitors for the last few months?"

"Oh, that's easy. She hardly had any visitors."

"But you keep records." He interjected.

Mrs. Botley bristled at his remark. "Of course we do! We run a professional home here, Inspector."

She turned on her heel. "I'll leave you to it, Inspector. I'm going to get the visitors' book."

The room fell silent, and Inspector Rawlings walked over to the tall wooden cabinet along the wall. He opened the glass-fronted doors and lifted a porcelain teacup off the shelf. It was hand-painted with delicate pink roses and gold leaf running around the rim. He turned it over to see the words "Royal Albert Camille" written on the base.

"Inspector!" Faye was standing in the doorway as he held the cup in his hand.

Turning, he frowned. "Miss Lantern, what are you doing here!?"

Taken aback by his curt tone, she stared blankly at him. "Well. I…"

"I thought I made it clear it was not safe to come here again!" He placed the cup back on the shelf. "For your own safety!"

Faye recomposed herself, "As Mrs. Penny is no longer with us, I saw no harm in coming." She said defiantly, watching him close the cabinet door.

Penny Townsend

He turned to look at her. "So, what are you doing here?"

She walked over to where he was standing and opened the cabinet door again.

"I received a call from Mrs. Botley yesterday, saying Mrs. Penny had left me the tea set I had been admiring when I was here." She picked up the cup he had been holding.

"This one. And the teapot and four cups and saucers."

Inspector Rawlings cast his eye over the teapot as she reached up.

"Let me." He took it down from the top shelf.

"I need to keep these all here until I've finished my investigation."

"Investigation?" she said, surprised.

His jaw tensed. "I'm investigating the murder of Mrs. Penny."

Faye gasped, putting her hand to her mouth as he continued.

"I received a call from the coroner this morning, confirming suffocation as the cause of death. It's likely she was smothered with her own pillow."

Noticing the shock on her face, he said,

"Would you like to take a seat, Miss Lantern? You look white as a sheet!"

Shaken, she walked over to the armchair to sit down.

"I was only here a few days ago." She looked down. "Sitting right here in this chair!" She gestured with her hand and stared at the armchair Mrs. Penny had been sitting in.

Secrets and Skeletons In The Teashop

"You were right, Inspector. I think Mrs. Penny must have known who the killer was."

Inspector Rawlings was now standing by the window, looking out across the harbor. His frown deepened.

"I wish I hadn't been." He spun on his heel as Mrs. Botley came back through the door with an ashen face.

"This is most serious, Inspector. Someone has torn out last week's visitors' page." She held out the sturdy leather book, opened at the missing page.

"Right here," she pointed. "The dates on the pages show the week before last and this week, but last week, on the 14th. The page is gone!"

She reached out for the arm of Mrs. Penny's high-backed chair and moved around to sit down, shaking her head from side to side.

"I will need to interview all your staff, Mrs. Botley, especially the ones on duty last week."

She nodded. "Of course, Inspector."

"This needs to be dealt with swiftly."

Mrs. Botley shook her head from side to side again as she looked at the torn book. "I can't believe it could be one of my staff."

"Let's not jump to any conclusions now. We'll let the evidence do the talking."

She stood up. "You are right, Inspector. I'll gather the staff now," and quickly left the room.

Faye admired the inspector's attitude to strive for the truth. She felt a growing closeness towards him that made her uneasy. It was new to her to not have control over her feelings, and her cheeks flushed as she spoke.

"Well, Inspector. No point in me hanging around."

A fleeting look of disappointment crossed his face.

"Yes. Absolutely Miss Lantern. I'm sure you have better things to do with your time."

After an awkward silence, he turned back to the visitors' book. Relief washed over her when she found herself back outside on the street. A welcome breeze rippled through her hair as she started the long walk home. A car horn beeping alongside her made her turn to see the door of a shiny, new Austin Healey swing open as the car stopped in front of her.

"Need a lift?"

Faye's whole body tensed as she saw Bill Green staring back at her. She forced a smile. "That's very kind of you, Bill, but I'm meeting Daniel." She looked at her watch. "He'll be here any minute."

He stared at her for a few seconds, which seemed like an eternity, as her heart thumped out of her chest. He nodded and, with a blank expression, leaned over, pulling the door shut before speeding off. She let out a sigh of relief. Inspector Rawlings' warning to be cautious still ringing in her ears, she continued walking home at a brisk pace.

Chapter Thirteen:
Mrs. Field

Mrs. Field's shrill voice carried across the road as Faye was walking out the tearoom door.

"Faye, cooee!" Waving, she walked and then trotted across the road, holding onto her hat as she stepped over a large puddle.

Half out of breath, she stopped in front of her. "Faye. I'm glad I caught you. I just thought you should know that Terrance Penny is in the village. He's in the pub right now, in fact."

Faye stared blankly at Mrs. Field, who sensed her confusion.

"The last time anyone saw him," she looked around and leaned in to whisper, "Was when Mr. Penny disappeared!" she straightened up, giving her a knowing look.

Faye, still bemused by the news, feigned a smile. "Thank you, Mrs. Field. I'll be sure to let Inspector Rawlings know he is in the village."

Mrs. Field threw her hands up in the air. "There's something that bumbling inspector wouldn't find if he stepped on it!"

Mrs. Field's grudge against the inspector was still as fresh as the day he arrested her, and she didn't care who knew it. She took a notebook out of her coat pocket.

"Tuesday," she said, peering down over her half-rimmed glasses. "At five o'clock in the morning, he was at Grimmers Point Quarry for two hours — Wednesday — six o'clock. He was there in the evening for four hours."

She ran her finger down the page. "It's been like that all week." She looked up over the top of her glasses, now perched on the end of her nose.

Faye glanced at the notebook. She knew Mrs. Field didn't have a dog to walk. "Five o'clock in the morning. You were at the quarry?"

Very matter of fact, she replied, "Of course! The birds are on the wing at sunrise."

"Birds? Mrs. Field. May I ask? Are you a twitcher, by any chance?"

Her eyes lit up as she spoke, "Oh, yes. Wilfred and I were always there early to take notes." Her face looked unusually soft as she spoke. "I miss him."

She suddenly straightened up. "And that's why I wanted to tell you about Terrance. Poor Wilf would be so upset! His concerns were justified!"

As Faye closed the tearoom door, she turned to her. "Concerns?" What do you mean? "

"He suspected Terrance of smuggling birds' eggs!" She pursed her lips into a point. "I saw him. He was walking with a climbing rope tied around his waist, and… he had a wooden box!"

Faye cast her mind back to the cave and the wooden box she had discovered with Inspector Rawlings.

"Do you know what was in the wooden box, Mrs. Field?"

Her thin, sharp nose screwed up in irritation. "I didn't see inside the box, but all the twitchers know what those wooden boxes are for. We look out for that kind of thing."

Secrets and Skeletons In The Teashop

Faye locked the tearoom door and put the key in her pocket. "I think you may have stumbled onto some important information, Mrs. Field. I would be happy to share it with Inspector Rawlings."

She turned her nose up again at the mention of his name. "Whatever you see fit. All I know is poor Wilf needs justice for what happened to him." And walked away.

Chapter Fourteen:
Under Suspicion

Inspector Rawling stood in Mrs. Botley's office, turning the pages of the visitors' book as she ushered in two women. A young, timid girl with her blonde hair tied in a ponytail, and an older woman in her fifties. She wore a starched white uniform, her steely grey hair pressed flat to her head.

"Inspector, this is Felicity," her hand held out in front of the young girl and then over to the older woman. And this is Patricia. Both were on duty the same day as the missing page accounts for. The young girl instantly broke down in tears, much to Mrs. Botley's annoyance.

"Pull yourself together, Felicity!"

Inspector Rawlings held out the visitors' book in front of them.

"Can either of you ladies tell me anything about this missing page?"

Patricia stood, arms folded across her chest, her broad Irish accent unmistakable as she said,

"Would you be accusing us of tearing out the page?" Her eyes locked on him, and he clenched his jaw, anger simmering beneath his calm exterior.

"Not at all, Patricia. I'm merely asking if you have any information to help me find out when the page was taken and by whom."

He placed the book down on the desk.

Secrets and Skeletons In The Teashop

"Let's start with the last time either of you filled in the book." He looked first at Patricia. "When was the last entry you wrote in the book?"

"Well, now. Let me see. I think it could have been the day before. To be sure now. It was Miss Lantern in the morning." His trained eye detected a hint of smugness as the corner of her mouth turned up momentarily.

He picked up the book and found the page. "There is no entry for Miss Lantern in here."

Patricia shrugged. "Ah, well now. I don't always get time to write in the visitors' book, being rushed off my feet, so I am. I can't go checking every little detail."

Clenching his jaw again before he spoke, he addressed her again.

"I'm asking you to think. Was there anyone else, any other visitor, that you omitted to write in the book?"

An uncomfortable silence fell in the room as Patricia raised her eyes up, subtly shaking her head from side to side.

Undeterred, he looked across at the young girl.

"Felicity?"

Felicity jumped as she heard her name.

"Can you tell me what you can remember about the 14th?"

She looked up nervously. Her eyes darting a sideways glance at Patricia. "Nothing, really. There were no visitors for Mrs. Penny that day that I saw." And looked down at the floor again.

Patricia nodded.

"Well, there you have it, Inspector. From the horse's mouth. To be sure, we have no idea about any missing pages. Would that be all you'll be wantin' from us? As we have chores a'waitin'."

Mrs. Botley glanced over at her. "Thank you, Patricia. But don't doubt the severity of this situation!"

Inspector Rawlings raised his hand. "It's okay, Mrs. Botley. I've finished for now."

Like a sprung coil let loose, she clapped her hands smartly together. "Quickly, ladies, back to work."

Inspector Rawlings sensed Felicity knew more than she was saying, and it would only be a matter of time before he found out.

Chapter Fifteen:
A Shocking Revelation

An array of orange and white flowers from yesterday's wedding adorned two golden stands, parading gloriously on either side of the aisle as Faye walked towards the pulpit. She took a candle from the box and stood at the altar. Lighting the candle, she placed it in its holder. The flame flickered in the breeze as she put it next to another candle already burning and stood back. She wanted to acknowledge Mrs. Penny's passing and fleetingly looked up.

"I hope you found Wilfred, Jane, and you are together and happy again."

Feeling better that she had at least said her goodbyes, she turned to leave when her heart jumped in her throat. The man from the cave was standing in front of her. Gasping, she staggered back. His menacing figure dressed all in black, stood out against the red of the aisle carpet. She held her breath as his narrowed eyes focused in on her. He looked pale and drawn, his long black hair tied into a ponytail. Drawing on a cigarette, he blew the smoke out, still staring at her.

"Why did you go visit my ma?"

It took a moment for her to register what he was asking.

"You're Terrance!"

His icy stare froze her to the spot, and fear ran through her as she avoided his gaze.

"I went to see Mrs. Penny, your mother, to let her know I was reopening the tearooms." She hesitated, searching his eyes for any hint of reaction that would ease her mind of his intentions. She was uncertain, and a nervous smile creased her mouth.

"I'm Faye Lantern. The new owner of the Station House." Her voice rose at the end, inviting him to reply. "Your mother mentioned you when I spoke to her. She seemed sad, as though she missed you."

The look in his eyes softened. "She said you had a good heart."

He gulped, tears glistening in his eyes before he turned his face slightly away.

"I'm sorry for your loss. But I know Inspector Rawlings will leave no stone unturned to find out who murdered her."

She felt a rush of fear as his expression suddenly changed. His face darkening.

"Murder?!"

Panic welled up inside her. "I'm so sorry, Terrance. I thought you knew."

His dark eyes flashed wildly in rage.

"How? How was she murdered?"

She felt her stomach knot as she gently tried to break the news.

"I believe someone smothered her with a pillow in the care home."

She prayed he wouldn't move any nearer as he lashed out, angrily kicking the flowers, sending them soaring through the air as the gold stand clattered on the floor. Without a backward glance, he turned, letting out a guttural roar, slamming the wooden door back into the wall as he strode out of the church.

Chapter Sixteen:
Drink Up

Faye tried shaking off the memory of her encounter with Terrance earlier that day as she pushed open the care home door. Walking along the corridor, it seemed unusually quiet. But maybe that's why Mrs. Botley had asked her to come so late in the day, so that she would have time without visitors there to help her collect the tea set Mrs. Penny had left her. Reaching Mrs. Botley's office, Faye tapped quietly on the opaque glass panel. Waiting, she turned her head and listened for any noise from inside, but everything was silent. She tapped again and called out.

"Mrs. Botley. It's Faye Lantern. I've come to collect the tea set."

She peered through the glass, her eyes searching for any movement. Realizing the office was empty; she walked down the hallway until she came to Mrs. Penny's old room. The door was ajar, and a soft light fell through the opening. She knocked on the door, and a lowered voice called out, "Come in."

Faye tentatively pushed the door open to see a grey-haired woman in a white nurse's uniform closing the cabinet with the tea set inside.

"Hello, I'm Faye. Mrs. Botley sent me a note to collect the tea set."

"Ah. So, you are. I've just been cleaning them. I thought we could have a cup of tea to send Mrs. Penny on her way. The pot's already filled. It's in the kitchen, so it is."

She hurried out of the room, not giving Faye a chance to reply. Bemused, Faye followed behind in the dimly lit corridor and entered the kitchen, where she found her pouring out the tea. She handed Faye a full cup and, picking up her own, let out a sneering laugh.

Penny Townsend

"To be sure, I don't think these cups have ever seen the light of day. There's not a scratch on them!"

Unsure what to make of her, Faye sipped her tea and studied the fine detail of the cup.

"These hand-painted roses are so beautiful. It's not surprising she didn't want to use them."

The nurse smirked. "I bet they're worth a pretty penny now."

Faye couldn't shake off an uncomfortable feeling she had and tried to lighten the mood.

"Did you know her before she came to the care home? Mrs. Penny, I mean."

She shot her a sharp glance. "We went way back," she paused. I'll let you into a little secret, so I will. I used to date Wilfred before Jane knew him—even introduced them." Her face had a slight tic under her eye, which quivered as she mentioned Wilfred.

"Of course, that's all in the past. They set up the tea shop and,"… she looked away, "had Terrance."

A moment passed before she turned back. "To be sure now, where are my manners? I'm Patricia."

Her tic was now more pronounced as she glanced at Faye. A self-satisfied smile suddenly curled the corner of her mouth up.

"That's right, dearie. Drink up."

"You know Terrance?" As the words left her mouth, her vision blurred, and her hand instinctively reached out for something to hold on to as her head grew foggy. The room suddenly began spinning, and she looked at Patricia in a panic.

Secrets and Skeletons In The Teashop

"What's happening?"

She felt the cup in her hand fall to the floor as her knees buckled, and Patricia faded from view before everything went dark.

Chapter Seventeen:
Patricia

Mrs. Field rang the Station House doorbell. She waited patiently, only to be disappointed when Daniel answered the door.

"Oh, it's you, Daniel. I would like to speak with Faye, please." Her hands clutched a wicker basket as she spoke.

"I'm afraid she's not home yet."

Mrs. Field looked at her watch and back at Daniel. "Not back home. It's ten to nine!"

Daniel tried to hide the growing concern he felt. Faye never went out at night without leaving a note to let him know where she was.

"I'm sure she will be back soon. Can I take a message for you?"

Mrs. Field hovered, then lifted her nose in the air. "Please tell Faye I need to speak with her urgently."

Daniel nodded. "I will let her know."

He closed the door with an uneasy feeling and walked down the hallway to the small table that the telephone sat on and lifted the receiver. Dialing the bakery, he was disheartened to hear that Gwen had no clue where Faye was. By the time ten o'clock arrived, he could feel panic rising within him as he picked up the telephone and called the police station.

Inspector Rawlings was just going off duty when he took the call and, within minutes, arrived at the Station House.

A worried Daniel opened the door, relieved to see the inspector standing there. "Inspector, I'm sure it's all fine, but I am getting

Secrets and Skeletons In The Teashop

concerned. Aunty Faye normally lets me know if she's going to be back late, but I haven't heard a thing from her."

Inspector Rawlings could see the frown lines on Daniel's forehead deepened.

"Now, Daniel. I'm sure it's nothing to worry about. Let's get some facts laid out. When exactly was the last time you spoke with her?"

Daniel's mouth pulled back, straining as he thought. "This morning. As I was leaving for work." He looked over at the mantelpiece clock. "That was fifteen hours ago!"

Inspector Rawlings kept his voice calm as he spoke.

"Did you check to see if she left a note?"

"She normally leaves one on the kitchen table. I'll double-check that it hasn't fallen on the floor or somewhere else. I didn't think to look anywhere else."

Daniel rushed into the kitchen as Inspector Rawlings walked into the dining room. His eyes glanced across their game of chess, still on the board. Looking around the room, an envelope caught his eye, lying open on the arm of Faye's chair by the fire.

The inspector walked in and picked up the letter. David's stomach dropped as he saw the inspector's anxious look as his eyes devoured the words in the letter. The inspector looked up at Daniel.

"This is from Mrs. Botley, asking Faye to pick up the tea set Mrs. Penny left her."

He folded up the letter and put it back in the envelope.

Daniel sighed with relief. "Well, that's good news, isn't it?"

Penny Townsend

He frowned. "I'm afraid not. The tea set is part of the ongoing investigation into Mrs. Penny's murder."

He placed the envelope inside his coat pocket. "Mrs. Botley knows that."

Daniel stared at him, tension filling his voice. "What are you saying?"

"I think, Daniel, someone other than Mrs. Botley has written this letter to Faye, and it's serious. There's no time to lose. I'm going to the care home now!"

He took a deep breath, trying to hold back the fear rising in him. "I'll come with you."

"No. It's better if you stay here. Just in case Faye comes back or calls you."

The inspector was right. Someone needed to be at the Station House in case Faye returned. He nodded.

"Don't worry, Daniel. I won't rest until Faye is safely back home. You have my word."

His tone was decisive and clear, but Daniel had an uneasy feeling in the pit of his stomach that Faye was in real trouble.

Chapter Eighteen:
Missing Without a Trace

Faye could feel the sharp pain of rocks pressing into her back as she lay on the ground, her eyes trying to focus on the dim light around her. She could just make out two figures, one walking towards her. Their voices faded as one of them turned back. She rolled on her side and sat up as Patricia stood in front of her.

"So, you'll be awake then." Her eyes narrowed. "You nearly upset my plans, dearie." She smiled a sickly half smile, and Faye sunk back against the uneven wall.

"Oh, I shan't be a hurting you yet. I've got plans for you."

Every bone in Faye's body filled with fear as Patricia leaned forward, inspecting the ropes that bound her wrists.

"So, I'll be needin' you to come with me now." She pulled at Faye's arm, lifting her up to her feet. "I have a little job that needs doin'."

She pushed Faye forward and her foot hit something solid on the floor. She could barely see in the dim light, but she recognized at once, she had kicked a wooden box, similar to the one she had discovered in the caves with Inspector Rawlings.

"Over here," she pulled at Faye's wrists until she was in the corner of the cave. The cold air made her shiver as she sank down to the floor.

"Why are you keeping me here?"

She didn't answer her and walked away, leaving Faye alone. A single candle flickered, her only comfort in the darkness.

....
....

Inspector Rawlings screeched to a halt outside the care home. He pulled his badge from the inside of his coat and rushed up the steps to ring the doorbell. A few minutes later, a nurse in her late forties opened the door. Her face bore an impatient air of authority. She was about to launch into a tirade about how she was too busy to be wasting her time with visitors who called after hours when he held his badge up.

"Inspector Rawlings, Sussex Police. I believe a crime has been committed here tonight. May I come in?"

Taken aback, she stared in astonishment at him as he placed his badge back in his pocket.

"It's extremely important. I need to come in immediately. Someone's life may be in danger!"

Blue flashing lights flooded the road as two police cars came into view and snapped her out of her stupor.

"Please, come in Inspector." She opened the door wide and stepped aside to let them in as Pemberley and the other policemen raced up the path behind him.

"Can you please tell me what is happening? I don't want the residents upset."

Inspector Rawlings beckoned his men forward. "I understand. May I ask your name?"

"Nurse Collins."

"Well, Nurse Collins. I have reason to believe someone lured Miss Lantern here under false pretenses. She has been missing for a few hours now, and I believe she may have been here today. Have you seen her?"

She took a sharp intake of breath, flustered.

"I only started my shift an hour ago. And I only saw Patricia."

Hearing Patricia's name, he tensed his jaw. "Where is Patricia now?"

"She's left. Her shift has ended."

Further along the corridor, Pemberley called out, making him turn around. "Over here, sir! I think I've found something," he said, disappearing back inside the room. He thanked Collins and raced down the corridor and into the weary-looking kitchen. His eyes scanned the room quickly as Pemberley held up a small, brown bottle.

"This was on the side here, by the kettle." A few tablets rattled around the bottle as Inspector Rawling tilted it to look inside.

"And look here, sir." He bent down and picked up a piece of a broken cup from under the table. He took it from Pemberley and instantly recognized the pattern from the teapot Faye had shown him earlier that day.

He looked over at the table. A single half-drunk cup of tea sat on a saucer. He wrapped his hand around the side of the cup — it was stone cold. His heart dropped. Valuable time had passed.

He nodded to Pemberley. "Bag this cup for forensics along with the broken cup pieces."

Nurse Collins walked into the room.

"Ah. Nurse Collins. Perfect timing. Can you tell me what these tablets are?" He held the bottle up.

Penny Townsend

She walked over, her eyes quickly scanning the bottle. "We give those to the residents if they are having trouble sleeping at night." Her face was now etched with concern.

"I don't understand why they are in here. They should be locked up in the medicine cupboard!"

He took the bottle from her and handed it to Pemberley.

"Thank you, Nurse Collins. You have been most helpful. Could you tell me, where is the rear exit door?"

He followed her to the back of the building and out into the small parking area.

Her eyes caught sight of a blue mini parked in the corner bay.

"That's odd! Patricia's car is still here!"

Chapter Nineteen:
An Unexpected Friend

Footsteps drawing closer made Faye look up. Peering into the darkness, her heart beating faster, she gasped as Terrance came into view. He stopped and stared at her as if shocked by her presence. Before he could say a word, someone came hurrying towards them, and he turned, leaving through the same hidden passageway he had disappeared through earlier that day as Patricia stood over Faye.

"I said I had a job for you. So, you'll be wantin' to get up."

The cold stiffened Faye's body, making her move slowly. She winced as Patricia's shoe hit the front of her shin.

"Hurry!"

She led her to the front of the cave, where a small wooden box with three eggs placed inside separate compartments was lying open on top of a large rock. Closing the lid, she handed the box to Faye and snarled, "Keep these eggs safe like your life depended on it."

Faye's hands shook as she picked up the box and held it close to her. They walked down the track in the moonlight until they reached a Morris van. She hadn't seen it in the village before and glanced at the number plate as she walked around to the rear passenger door.

"In the front," Patricia growled.

Faye carefully maneuvered into the front seat of the van, clutching the box, her heart pounding as Patricia sat down in the driver's seat next to her. She had no idea why she was holding her prisoner or where they were going as she watched Patricia turn the key and fire up the engine.

Penny Townsend

They drove slowly down the unmade road and after a few miles, Patricia sped up as she turned onto a side road. Faye screamed as a man wearing a hooded coat jumped out in front of them, making Patricia swerve, crashing the van headfirst into the hedge that flanked the road. In a heartbeat, the van door opened, and Faye felt herself being pulled back into her seat. Terrance was standing there and, in one swift move, pulled the box she was still holding on to from her hands and said, "Get out."

She hesitated. Patricia was lying back in her seat, a small trickle of blood running down her face.

"What about Patricia?"

Terrance's face darkened, "Leave her."

Faye stepped out of the van, her body shaking as Terrance stood in front of her.

"Follow the path to the end. There's a cottage. Wait there!"

Unsure it was safe, she looked down the unmade path. She could make out a faint light in the distance. A car's headlights behind them swung into view, lighting up the end of the road, and Terrance cussed under his breath.

He turned back sharply to her, "Go!"

………………………………………………………………………
………………………………………………………………………

Inspector Rawling stood outside Patricia's house, his hands cupped around his eyes, peering in through the window into the darkened living room.

Pemberley walked back around the house. "There's no one home. I've checked the back door. It's locked, and there's no sign of any movement inside."

Secrets and Skeletons In The Teashop

His jaw clenched as he stood back and looked up at the windows. Everything was in darkness. "Get someone over to Miss Lantern's house to see if she has returned."

As he spoke, he knew his words were as empty as the chances of finding Faye safely back at the Station House—but he had to check.

Chapter Twenty:
The Cottage

Faye's hands reached out in the darkness for the cottage door. She leaned her shoulder into the wooden panels as she pushed down on the metal handle, praying it would move. She staggered forward as the door lurched open. A faint light shone out further down the hall, and she trod softly in the darkness towards the light. As she neared the open door, she jumped as a telephone rang out. She gasped, putting her hand to her mouth as she saw Bill Green answer the telephone. She stepped back, leaning against the wall, her heart beating loudly as she stood in the shadows.

"Yes. I'll make my way there now." He slammed the receiver down.

She let out a sigh of relief as she heard the back door slam behind him. She waited a few moments, listening, and hearing his car pull away, crept into the lounge, lit only by a single lamp in the window. The telephone sat on a small side cabinet. Picking up the receiver, she noticed a crack in the glass of her watch. It must have broken in the accident. She would get it fixed when she got back home. The mere thought of the Station House sent tears rolling down her cheeks again. She missed Daniel and Buster, but her heart ached more than ever for Inspector Rawlings, wishing he would appear before her and wrap his arms around her. She sobbed as she dialed the police station. Listening to the telephone ringing, she twisted the coiled lead in her fingers, her stomach twisting in bouts of anxiety.

"Please pick up." After a few minutes of desperately waiting with no reply, she disconnected the call. Trembling, she dialed the Station House.

She burst into tears as she heard Daniel's desperate voice say,

Secrets and Skeletons In The Teashop

"Aunty Faye?"

"Yes." She gasped, taking a deep breath. "I need help."

Panic rose in his voice. "Where are you?"

She wiped tears away from her eyes with the back of her hand as she looked around.

"I'm in a cottage. It has leaded windows, and I can hear the sea close by. It's near a cave." As she explained to Daniel, it suddenly dawned on her. "I think it's by Grimmer Point! …… Daniel, Daniel."

She pressed the receiver, but the line had gone dead. Headlights flashing through the lounge window lit up the room as she heard a car screech to a halt outside. She ran behind the sofa as footsteps came rushing down the hallway. Crouching down in silence as someone walked in. She screamed as Bill Green pulled the sofa away and stood in front of her.

"Why did you have to tell Terrance? Now you've made things difficult! Come with me." He ordered, grabbing her by the arm.

As they walked outside, he turned on a torch to light their way.

"Don't bother screaming or shouting. No one's going to hear you. There's not another house about these parts for miles."

Reaching the end of the track, they approached the van, still stuck headfirst in the hedge. Anxiety took hold as her eyes searched for any sign of Patricia inside, but the van was empty.

She looked over at Bill, "Where is Patricia?"

His breathing was heavy from the walking. He nodded, "Up a ways."

Penny Townsend

Dread filled her at the thought of seeing her again.

"What about Terrance?"

"Long gone, I hope for his sake."

They continued walking for another mile before finally reaching the cave entrance.

Patricia was standing there waiting for them. Her face was red and swollen, with a jagged cut under her eye. She glared menacingly at Faye as Bill pushed her into the edge of the cave and, grabbing her chin in her hand, narrowed her eyes.

"So, you thought you could run away?"

Faye held her breath, terrified to move for what seemed like an eternity before Patricia suddenly pulled her hand away.

"To be sure, you're only still here because I have a need for you."

She looked at Bill, "Is everything ready?"

"No. We have a problem."

Chapter Twenty-One:
Desperate Measures

It was four o'clock in the morning when Daniel telephoned Inspector Rawlings in a panic.

"Inspector. Faye called. She thinks she is somewhere near Grimmer Point. She was so distraught."

Daniel's words hit him like a sucker punch to the gut. He clenched his jaw, gripping the receiver so tight his knuckles went white. He knew Faye wouldn't venture out on her own to the cliffs.

"Did she say how she got there or who was with her?"

"No. We got cut off before she could say too much. She mentioned a cottage by the sea and... oh...near caves."

A picture started forming in his head of the path that led from the caves at Grimmer Point to 'Sea Salter cottage.' Without a car, he knew Faye could not get there alone.

"I'm going there now," he said abruptly and put the receiver.

....
....

The sun was rising as he arrived with Pemberley at the cliffs.

"You take the path up to the top, and I'll head along the track to the cave."

After thirty minutes, Pemberley came down through a gap in the rocks, entering the caves through a series of narrow walls, finally appearing in front of the inspector, who was kneeling on the ground next to a large flat rock.

"See here, Pemberley. Three sets of footprints lead out of the cave. They weren't here the other day when I was with,…" he gulped, Faye's name catching in his throat. He stood up and looked around. "And it looks like someone stayed here." He pointed to the melted candle wax that had dripped down the rock.

Car doors slamming interrupted his thoughts as more of his men arrived. Although tiredness had crept into his bones, he wouldn't let the trail go cold. After directing his men to spread out along the cliff and make a thorough search of the rock face, he jumped in his car, followed closely behind by Pemberley. They drove along the road, headed to the 'Sea Salter' cottage. All the while, his mind turned over, trying to piece things together, when he slammed on his brakes.

A truck that had crashed headfirst into the hedge came into view. Skidding to a halt, he rushed out of the car and over to the truck, his stomach churning, dreading what he might find. To his relief, the car was empty. The windscreen hanging over the bonnet was a sign the car had been speeding upon impact. He looked around and saw the unmade road now leading to the cottage, barely visible in the distance. Racing back to his car, he flew along the track and pulled up at the cottage, which was perched dangerously close to the eroding cliff face. He desperately wanted to find Faye safely inside. The back door was wide open, and his heart sank as he searched, calling her name before realizing the house was empty. Pemberley rushed in, out of breath.

"They've cut the telephone lines outside."

Coupled with the sofa being pulled out into an otherwise perfectly tidy room, Inspector Rawlings could piece together that it was possible Faye called Daniel from the telephone at the cottage. And maybe hid behind the sofa to avoid detection. But the position of the sofa suggested they had found her. His stomach lurched at the thought of any harm coming to her.

Secrets and Skeletons In The Teashop

Over the next few hours, he swept the cliffs and surrounding areas with his men and failed to find anything that could place Faye at the scene. Reluctantly, he called off the search and broke the news to Daniel, impressing upon him that it was only for a few hours, then he would resume the search and the investigation.

Chapter Twenty-Two:
Childhood Memories

Gwen had just opened the bakery when Daniel called on the telephone. Shocked by the news, she took a sharp breath.

"We have to do something. We have to try."

"Inspector Rawlings isn't stopping, Gwen. I think we should hang on."

She nodded silently to herself. "But we could at least get a search party organised."

Part of Daniel wanted to agree with her, but he knew it could interfere and even jeopardise Faye's safety if they impeded the investigation.

"I really think you should talk to the inspector first. You don't want to go trampling on evidence, or worse still, get caught up with some sinister characters and make even more trouble!"

As if deaf to Daniel's words of wisdom, she straightened her back. "If you ask me, I think Bill Green is mixed up in all this!"

Daniel's eyebrows furrowed, "What makes you say that?"

"He met Terrance in the tearoom on the day the cyclists were there. I didn't recognise him at first. It's been years since I've seen him. But he was with him. They were in the corner, and there were mysterious pieces of straw on the table where they were sitting."

"Have you told Inspector Rawlings?"

Secrets and Skeletons In The Teashop

"Oh, Tom was in the tearoom when I noticed it. He must have made the connection as he rushed out on business once he saw the straw."

Daniel suddenly remembered the conversation he had with Faye about the rare birds' eggs being poached. Knowing Faye could have inadvertently gotten caught up in it made him feel sick with fear.

"This is a horrible business. Maybe we could put our heads together and at least try to come up with something useful to help the investigation."

Gwen pumped the air with her hand, thrilled to get Daniel agreeing to try something.

"Yes! Can you come over to the bakery now?"

After a moment of silence on the telephone, he said. "I'll call work to let them know I'm taking a few days' holiday, and I'll be right over."

Gwen already had tea and cakes laid out when Daniel came through the bakery door. She led him to the parlor, and he sat down on the chair uneasily.

Pouring out the tea, she pushed a cup over to Daniel. The mood somber, she said, "Do you think Faye is in danger?"

He blinked slowly, the curves of his mouth drawn back in fear at the reality of the situation. "I think she could be in real danger."

Gwen sat up straight. "Well, there's no time to lose, then! What do we know so far?"

"I think it has something to do with Grimmer Point and smuggling birds' eggs."

She watched Daniel grip the handle of the teacup so tightly that she thought it would break in two.

"What do you mean, smuggling birds' eggs?"

"Well, the other day, Faye came home and was talking about Grimmer Point and finding a wooden box."

He looked crestfallen. "I told her it may have been for smuggling the eagles' eggs."

Gwen suddenly became animated. "Of course! Why didn't I think of it before? It all fits. Bill Green and Wilfred were twitchers! The straw on the table at the tearoom, and then meeting Terrance."

She thought for a moment. "You know, when we were young, Tom, me, and Terrance all used to play down by the cliffs at Grimmer Point. There was an old shack there—we had a camp in." She smiled, recalling childhood memories.

"Terrance was always climbing the cliffs and trees and stealing eggs from birds' nests. He would come over all proud of himself, but I told him off, of course, and made him put them back. If Terrence has anything to do with it, then maybe we should look down by the shack."

Daniel sat up and straightened his back. "Hang on a minute, Gwen. Don't you think we should tell Inspector Rawling first?"

Gwen raised her hand, brushing his comment away.

"Let's not bother the inspector just yet. We could just look from the cliff and not go any further."

Seeing the look of uncertainty on Daniel's face, she said,

"It won't do any harm — and Faye needs us!"

Secrets and Skeletons In The Teashop

Daniel sighed, remembering how desperate Faye sounded on the telephone.

"As long as we only look, and if we see anything," he stressed. "We'll call the inspector straight away."

Gwen nodded. "It's a deal! Let's go then."

"What now?"

"Yes! You said you took the day off!"

Daniel could think of a million ways he would rather spend his day off than looking for nefarious sorts at an old shack, but Faye was in danger, and her kindness towards him had been life-changing. Without her help, he would not be restarting his life in the village. He put his cup down.

"Let's do it."

Seizing the moment. Gwen jumped up, pulling her apron off and calling out to Tina. "I'll be back in a while." And rushed out the door with Daniel close behind.

Chapter Twenty-Three:
Finders Keepers

Patricia glared at Bill. "What problem?"

He took his cap off and rubbed his head nervously with his hand. "After the crash, the eggs disappeared!"

Patricia turned to Faye. "So, you think you're playin' games, do you?"

Faye stepped back in fear. She didn't want her to know about Terrence letting her go. Despite being mixed up in all of this, he had a good heart.

"I left the van and ran to the cottage." Her mind instantly jumped to the phone call she made to Daniel.

"I left the box on the floor of the van."

Patricia lifted the back of her hand up towards Faye's face when Bill said.

"It was Terrance. I saw him running down the path to Hollows End on my way to the cottage. He was carrying the box."

Only the tick, quivering under Patricia's eye, moved as she stared at Bill. "So, he thinks he's hit the jackpot and is going to take all the money for himself now." She shoved Faye forward.

"Get her into the car. We'll be taking a little visit to see Terrance, so we will. And…." She looked at Bill. "Make sure you're prepared!"

Bill reached inside his jacket and pulled out a small handgun. With a sickly smile, she turned to look at Faye, nodding her approval.

Secrets and Skeletons In The Teashop

....
....

Faye felt like all the energy to move had left her body as she sat in the passenger seat of Bill's car. Recalling the phone call, she was sure Daniel heard her before the line went dead.

Out of the window, a worn-out shack came into view. Close to the sea, its greying wooden timbers aged and blended into the background of the open quarry and nearby trees.

"Here!" Patricia shouted from the back seat.

"Pull in here. Where no one can see us."

Bill turned the car, parking short of the cliff's face and far enough back that they could climb down the path unseen to the shack below.

It was a treacherously steep descent down the side of the cliff. There were a few wooden steps, remnants of a time when the quarry workers used them as a cut-through down to the shack. The rotting steps now moved like marbles underfoot as they tried to pick their way around them. Her hands still tied, Faye looked down at the sheer drop to the rocks below, making her tip forward, sliding out of control. Gasping in terror, she lunged out, grabbing an overhanging tree branch perilously close to the edge. Relief swept over her as she steadied herself. At the bottom, Patricia stood in silence, taking in the area. Everywhere looked like an empty wasteland, with sweeping winds pushing the tufts of seagrass as they bent forward onto a vast expanse of sand dunes leading onto the shore. In any other situation, it could have been an idyllic retreat. A door banging in the wind drew all their attention over to the shack. Patricia's eyes scanned for any movement.

"There!" Bill shouted. "He's making a run for it!"

Penny Townsend

In the distance, Faye could see the back of Terrance's black leather jacket as he ran like the wind, headed towards the forest of cypress trees behind the shack.

"Get after him, Bill!"

Patricia pushed Faye forward as Bill took off running, letting off a couple of shots in Terrance's direction, but by the time he had reached the tree line, Terrance was long gone, and he stopped, bent over with his hands on his knees, gasping for air as Patricia caught up.

"Don't just stand there! Keep going, will you? He'll be a'hidin' in there somewhere. I want those eggs!"

He straightened up and took off again as Patricia opened the shack door and pushed Faye inside.

Chapter Twenty-Four:
A Chance Encounter

Daniel felt every bump in the road as they headed to 'Hollow's End.'

"What If we find Faye and something dreadful has happened?"

Gwen tried to calm his nerves. "Of course, nothing bad has happened. Faye knows what she's doing." She looked away and, for the first time, felt fearful for Faye.

Wishing he had her optimism, Daniel peered through the car windscreen, taking in the cliff top and vast expanse of blue sky as they came to a stop.

Gwen looked over towards the far end of the Ridge.

"Isn't that Bill Green's car?"

Daniel felt stricken with fear. "Let's just go back and get the inspector."

Gwen had already jumped out and was heading towards the car as he stumbled after her.

"Wait, Gwen. It could be dangerous!"

Gwen, deaf to his protest, could see no one was inside the car. "It's safe! There's no one here!"

She tried the handle, and the door opened. Daniel looked around, mortified.

"What are you doing?"

Penny Townsend

"Searching for clues."

A glint caught her eye as she looked down at the footwell of the front passenger seat. Moving pieces of dry straw out of the way, her hand found the silver strap of a watch; its glass face cracked down the middle.

She gasped. "This is Faye's watch!"

Daniel took it from her and turned it over, frowning as he saw the damaged glass. A sickening nausea crept over him.

"I hope she is okay."

Gwen walked around the car. "There's no sign of any damage."

Two gunshots in quick succession rang out in the distance, making them both jump. Edging cautiously towards the cliff edge, they peered down below and saw Patricia pushing Faye into the shack as a man wielding a gun ran through the woods and out of view.

"Faye!" Gwen screamed.

Daniel instantly grabbed her, putting his hand over her mouth, and pulled her to the ground. "Be quiet!"

Patricia stopped and looked up, scanning the clifftop. She waited a few seconds, listening, and then disappeared inside the shack. Daniel let out a sigh of relief as Gwen, heart pumping, pushed him away and shouted.

"What do you think you're doing!? We need to get down there and rescue Faye!"

Daniel raised his eyes up in disbelief as they lay side by side. "There's a mad gunman firing Willy Nilly in the woods, and Patricia looks like she could take us both down! No. Not today,

Secrets and Skeletons In The Teashop

thank you! We had a deal — remember? We would get Inspector Rawlings straight away if we found anything."

Seeing the coast was clear, they both scrambled to their feet. Daniel brushed the dirt from his trousers and shirt.

Gwen stared at him and then back to the shack. "But we can't leave Faye!"

Daniel, frustrated, shook his head. "I love Aunty Faye more than words can say, but we could get captured, too, and there's no good ending to that outcome!... Let's get Inspector Rawlings."

He rushed back to the car, and Gwen, realizing she couldn't go alone, followed him like a petulant child unable to get her own way.

"Well, at least don't drive like a Nancy! — Especially when Faye's life might depend on it!"

Daniel jumped into the car.

"I'll forget you said that!" And sped off full pelt, leaving a terrified Gwen hanging on to the car seat for all she was worth.

Chapter Twenty-Five: Hollow's End

Back in the village, Daniel drove straight to the police station. Red-faced and out of breath, he rushed up to the desk sergeant.

"Inspector Rawlings! I need to speak with Inspector Rawlings. It's an emergency!"

The desk sergeant spoke slowly.

"Now, Daniel. It is Daniel, isn't it? Faye Lanterns' nephew?"

"Yes. But please, I need to......"

The Sergeant interrupted him. "Calm down, Daniel, and tell me what has happened."

Fraught, Daniel said again. "I need to speak with Inspector Rawlings!"

The sergeant stood tall, raising his head up as he spoke. "I'm afraid he's not at his desk at the moment. He's out on an investigation."

Daniel was thrown. He had expected to speak with Inspector Rawlings.

The Sergeant continued. "Can you tell me what has happened, Daniel?"

"Yes. Er... Well. We tracked down my aunt Faye, who had gone missing. Someone has kidnapped her! We saw her at the shack at 'Hollows End.'"

"When was this?" He said, now more serious.

Secrets and Skeletons In The Teashop

"About twenty minutes ago. We drove straight here."

"We?" He inquired.

"Yes. I was with Gwen from the bakery."

The Sergeant nodded. "And what makes you think they kidnapped your aunt?"

"We saw her being shoved into the shack by an older grey-haired woman who was wearing a nursing-type uniform. And…" he added.

"There was a man firing a handgun, running in the woods by the shack!"

The desk sergeant puffed out his chest with authority.

"Hollows End, you say?"

"Yes. Please hurry. Faye is in danger." Sweat, now running down his face, he lifted his arm and wiped it with his sleeve.

"Rest assured, Daniel, we will deal with it immediately. Go home and wait. I'll get the inspector to call you when we have more information."

Daniel hesitated, wanting to say he would go there with them, but he knew he could do no more and left the station.

………………………………………………………………………
………………………………………………………………………

Inspector Rawlings hardly slept the few hours he had stopped searching for Faye. The telephone ringing made him shout out in his sleep, waking him up.

"Yes."

"It's Pemberley. Sorry to wake you up, Sir, but I thought you should know Miss Lantern's nephew came into the police station to report a sighting of her at Hollows End."

Rubbing his eyes, the Inspector's mind raced back to childhood days spent there. He suddenly sat up.

"When was this?"

"About fifteen minutes ago. He said he saw Miss Lantern going into the old shack...." He hesitated. "But it seems the description of the woman she was with fits our description of Patricia Derry, and Daniel has reason to believe she is holding Miss Lantern there against her will."

Panic flooded his mind. Patricia's fingerprints were on the bottle of sleeping pills and the teacups he had collected from the care home.

"Can you get Daniel to come down to the station? I'm on my way."

"Yes, Sir. Right away."

In a flurry of activity, he got dressed and rushed out the door, trying to focus only on his job. But no matter how hard he tried to ignore it, his mind kept drifting back to Faye, and the moment he could take her in his arms, he was in love with her.

Daniel was already at the police station when Inspector Rawlings came rushing in the door.

"Daniel! Good! This way."

They walked into his office and Daniel sat down as Pemberley handed Inspector Rawlings a typed statement from Daniel's earlier conversation. He skimmed through it quickly and looked up.

Secrets and Skeletons In The Teashop

"You saw Faye. How was she? Did she seem okay?"

Daniel's heartbeat quickened as his mind recalled the events.

"She was so far away — it was difficult to see properly. But she walked, or rather was pushed into the shack by a grey-haired woman."

Inspector Rawlings put the statement down.

"That grey-haired woman fits our description of Patricia Derry. We believe she may have drugged Faye and abducted her." He paused….

"She is also the prime suspect in the murders of Wilfred and Jane Penny."

Daniel's mouth fell open.

"We have to get Faye out of there."

Inspector Rawling's eyes flashed with determination.

"I have men ready and waiting. We have to show caution. You said you heard gunshots, so I've called in armed officers."

He stood up as Pemberley put his head around the door and nodded to him. He looked at Daniel.

"We're leaving now!"

Concern for Faye outweighed Daniel's fear. In a fit of momentary courage, he blurted out, "I'll come with you!"

"No, Daniel! You need to stay here. It's too dangerous."

Daniel nodded and slowly followed him out the door. Walking to the car, he realized Inspector Rawlings was going above and beyond to get Faye back to safety, and he was secretly relieved not to see Hollows End again. Opening the car door, he saw Gwen rushing towards him.

"There you are Daniel. I've been trying to call you."

"Oh. For what?"

"I've had a brainwave!"

"No," he said instantly. "God forbid, whatever it is, it will probably involve me ending up injured at the bottom of a cliff somewhere."

Gwen rolled her eyes. "Don't be so dramatic, Daniel. I just thought we could take Buster to Hollows End."

He frowned, "What on earth for?"

"To track them."

Thinking she had completely lost her mind, he said, "But we know where they are?"

Drawing out her words, she said, "Yes……... but………. what if they have already left when Tom gets there?"

He shook his head. "Even if that were to happen, they have police dogs for that kind of thing."

He got into the car and started the engine. "I've got to go!" he shouted.

And took off, leaving Gwen standing there before she could throw any more outlandish ideas at him. Hoping, above all else, that

Secrets and Skeletons In The Teashop

Inspector Rawlings would find Faye at Hollows End and bring her back safely.

Chapter Twenty-Six:
The Shack

There was no time to lose as Inspector Rawlings sped along the lanes, heading towards Hollows End. His men followed behind. He thought about the layout of the nearby areas. He wanted to get down to the shack unnoticed and ordered the men to pull up quietly at the beginning of the lane. On foot and his mind on Faye, they hurried down the track. He spoke quietly, directing his men to take the old path down the quarry pit and spread out, surrounding the shack at the bottom.

As they got into position, he crouched down. There was no movement from inside — no telltale shadows through the windows. He waved his men forward to surround the shack. Pemberley rushed ahead and smashed the door open with one kick, another officer right behind him. Inspector Rawlings ran in, and his heart sank immediately as his eyes scoured the room. Faye was not there. The shack was empty except for an old wooden table and two chairs — a memory from his childhood days and a newspaper lying on top. Picking it up, he saw yesterday's date. He threw it back down.

"There's nothing here!"

He stormed out into the cool air and took a deep breath. For the first time in his career, he had failed. Faye was still in danger, and he felt powerless. There were no clues. The cabin had been clean, except for the paper that showed him they were there. Frustrated, he kicked a rock across the gravel. This wasn't how he had envisioned it. He clenched his jaw. Patricia seemed to be one step ahead of him, and the more time Faye was missing, the graver danger she was in.

"Pemberley!" He shouted. "Look for tracks along the gravel and sand. Look for anything out of place on the paths."

Secrets and Skeletons In The Teashop

Pemberley, always efficient and ready to serve, jumped into action.

"Yes, sir!" And gathered the men, sending them in different directions.

Inspector Rawlings looked towards the forest behind the shack.

"With me, Pemberley." Who started running to catch up with the inspector, reaching him at the edge of the forest.

"You go left, and I'll take the right." He looked at his watch. "We'll meet back here in an hour."

Pemberley nodded and took off, heading south. The inspector heading north. He knew the woods well from playing there as a child and remembered the path that led down to one of the Manor House cottages. The path ended at the white cottage garden gate. He walked through, his eyes scouring the low-level trees and shrubs, looking for broken branches on the ground or evidence of footprints left behind in the dirt. By the time he reached the side gate, the trail had gone cold. He cursed out loud.

The walk back through the forest was arduous. As he arrived back, he barked orders at his men to disband after discovering there was still no evidence. His focus now sharp, determined to track Patricia down, he called out to Pemberley.

"Terrance Penny's house. Let's go!"

....
....

Daniel put the receiver down, still in shock. He thought it was all over, that Faye would come walking through the Station House door any minute with Inspector Rawlings. The reality was she was still in danger. He walked into the kitchen when the telephone rang again, and he ran back into the hall, hoping it would be good news from the inspector.

"Daniel. It's Gwen! They haven't found Faye!"

Daniel's stomach churned into a knot. He was reluctant to agree with anything she said for fear of being lured into another catastrophic plan.

"The inspector is still searching and doing all he can."

"Well, I think we should take Buster back to Hollows En and see if we can pick up the trail."

Every fibre in Daniel's body wanted to protest against Gwen's idea, but he found himself thinking it through.

"Come on, Daniel. Buster is the best at tracking, and if we find anything, anything at all, we'll go back and tell Tom. It will be the same deal we made earlier."

After a few moments of silence, he sighed. "Alright. I'll pick you up in five minutes." Already regretting the decision before he replaced the receiver back down.

Chapter Twenty-Seven:

Buster

All the way to Gwen's, Daniel convinced himself that this was a bad idea. By the time he pulled up at the bakery, Gwen was standing outside, waiting. She opened the car door and looked in.

"Oh, Buster, you good boy." She reached over to the back seat to pat him.

Daniel gripped on tightly to the steering wheel with one hand, the other poised on his brow.

"Gwen. I'm having heart palpitations. Maybe this isn't such a good idea."

Ignoring him, she slammed the car door shut. "Oh, nonsense. We're ready, aren't we, Buster?" She said, turning to pat him again.

"Come on, Daniel. Let's go!"

Reluctantly, he drove off, his mind racing to all the worst possible outcomes.

"What if we see them again?"

Gwen stifled a laugh.

"I hope we do. That's the whole point of going!"

"I mean," he stammered. "What if we see them and they see us.... How fast can you run?"

Gwen sighed. "Let's just get there and let Buster do his job."

They continued in silence, Buster dribbling over Daniel's shoulder as they turned into Hollows End. Gwen raced out of the car, followed by a reluctant Daniel, who was being dragged full pelt by Buster. They started down the Cliff to the quarry. At the bottom, Daniel started walking aimlessly about with Buster on the lead, desperately trying to pull him in a different direction.

"Well. That's that. Buster hasn't found anything."

Gwen walked over and snatched the lead from him.

"Come on, Buster!" He took off with Gwen, running behind him, heading straight for the shack. The door was still open from Inspector Rawling's earlier visit, and Buster ran with his head down, sniffing along the floor, and let out a bark. Faye had been sitting in the corner, out of view from the window. Buster kept his nose to the ground, following Faye's scent out of the shack. Gwen, trying to keep up with him again, as he raced across the stone beach and stopped. He stood barking, looking out to sea.

Daniel reached them, gasping, and looked out to sea as Buster continued to bark.

"I can't see anything." Panic suddenly washed over him. "You don't think…" he stared at the waves rolling in as Gwen finished his sentence.

"That she drowned? No! But I know you can sail a boat around the bay from here."

Daniel, horrified at the suggestion, gazed out at the sea again. "It's out of the question. I get terribly seasick!" He looked around. "And anyway, there are no boats around. So that's that."

Gwen's eyes lit up, and Daniel immediately panicked.

"Oh no. No. No!"

Secrets and Skeletons In The Teashop

She smiled. "My ex has a fishing boat moored close by. I'm sure he'll lend a hand when he knows what's at stake. Come on, Buster."

Daniel stood his ground. "Gwen, we made a deal, remember? We would contact Inspector Rawlings."

"Of course." She called back. "But we haven't found anything yet!"

He went to protest again when Gwen raised her hand to stop him. "I know what you are going to say, and I've already thought ahead. When we reach the boatyard, we can use the telephone to call Tom."

Daniel's face fixed in a stern pose, ready to argue, suddenly relaxed.

"Fine. The telephone, I'm agreeing to, but nothing else."

Gwen's eyes glistened. "Of course!"

....
....

The boatyard was fairly quiet as they pulled up. An elderly fisherman in a black cap and waterproofs was carrying lobster pots off a boat and disappeared behind a ramshackle wooden shed. Daniel waited by the car with Buster as Gwen went into the yard office. Five minutes later, she came out with a tall, dark-skinned man wearing a cable knit jumper sporting a beard. His bright orange and green Rasta hat covered his dreadlocks. He looked about as far from the image of a Naval Captain Daniel had envisioned in his head as could be. They walked side by side. Reaching Daniel, he smiled. His teeth were as dazzling white as the chalk cliff. He held out his hand.

"Olly!" Daniel Felt at ease the instant he shook his hand.

"Daniel!"

Gwen reached for Buster's lead. "I've called the station and left a message for Tom to let him know where we are heading. Come on." She said, turning and walking away. "Olly is taking us to the bay."

Daniel instantly wretched at the thought of going on the boat and out to sea.

"Wait!" he called out, running after them.

Olly was walking down the jetty, with Gwen and Buster close behind him. Daniel stopped as Olly jumped on the boat and held out his hand to Gwen, who stepped on with Buster. They all turned and stood looking at him. Buster barked twice, waiting as Olly started the engine, and Daniel watched the boat dip up and down.

"Oh, dear God!"

He ran swiftly down the jetty and jumped on, clinging on to the side for dear life as they sailed out to sea.

Chapter Twenty-Eight:
The Last Time

Bill ran down the bay and climbed onto the boat, moored out of sight of the cliffs. He had lost Terrance in the woods, and there was no time left to pursue him. The tide would turn soon, and he needed to get the boat ready. Patricia's voice cut through the silence.

"Bill!"

He had known Patricia from his days as a delivery driver. She worked in the greengrocers, and he would look forward to their daily chats until he eventually asked her out on a date. They would talk about their lives, and she was clear - she wanted more out of life than just being a shop assistant - that's when she found out about the eagles' eggs. She saw an opportunity to make enough money to break free and start their own business. He had argued at first, but eventually, she wore him down. And now he was in too deep to turn back.

"Over here," he called out.

Faye winced in pain, the sores on her feet burning, cut from the sand in her shoes, rubbing into open wounds. She stopped and, slipping off her shoes, rubbed her feet. The path down to the Bay was sandy, and she at least could get some relief from the pain.

Patricia pushed her from behind her, "Get a move on."

She sighed and carried on, not stopping until she reached the bay below. Dropping onto the sand, she took a deep breath in and sighed again, relaxing as the pain from her feet eased. She watched the Seagulls whirl above their heads, calling out as they drifted high above them.

She could see Bill emerge from the cabin of the boat. For the first time, Patricia left her alone to sit on the sand. She had nowhere to go, only back up, and they would catch her easily if she made a run for it. She overheard Patricia asking to see the eggs. Terrance, in his panic to leave the shack, left the eggs behind. He would have known Bill carried a gun if they had been working together, and he wasn't hanging around or going to be slowed down carrying the box as he escaped. It probably saved his life. She watched Patricia open the box, her eyes greedily devouring the eggs, touching them carefully before shutting the lid and handing them back to Bill. She turned to her.

"You'll be needin' to get on the boat now."

Faye didn't want to move. She wanted to escape from her. She looked around at the steep climb, back up the path again, and, as if sensing her thoughts, Bill jumped off the boat and came striding towards her. He watched Patricia walk away, then turned back to Faye.

"Let's not make a fuss. I find it's easier that way."

"Why are you keeping me here?" she said, desperate to understand why Patricia had taken her with them.

Bill stared at her long enough for her to realise he was deliberating what to say. "You're needed to make an exchange in Terrance's place."

"What are you telling her!?" Patricia shouted out. "Just bring her over!"

He reached down and put his arm under hers, helping her to stand, and she hobbled in pain across the sand to the boat.

"Where are we going?"

Patricia smirked. "You'll see."

Secrets and Skeletons In The Teashop

Bill pulled up the anchor and started the engine, turning the boat and slowly building up speed until they were racing across the open sea. Her hair flying back in the wind was a momentary relief as she watched the Bay disappear from view. The boat flew along, every few seconds hitting a wave and jumping up before the whirr of the engine finally slowed down.

A towering white lighthouse came into view and disappeared again as Bill steered the boat around the cove and alongside the wooden platform. He threw out a rope as Patricia stepped off. Quickly grabbing the rope, she wrapped it tightly around the post to secure the boat. Bill turned off the engine and disappeared into the cabin. A few seconds later, he re-emerged with the wooden box, handing it to Patricia. He held out his hand to Faye as she moved in time with the dip and sway of the boat and stepped off onto the platform.

She followed Patricia up the rocky path and into the lighthouse, shutting the door behind her as Bill walked over and started making a fire in the stove. The room was appealing in its own way. A sofa and chairs sat comfortably next to a large black stove, and a small kitchen nestled just to the side. An old book lay lying open on a desk, with a window above that looked out to sea. She sat down on a chair by the stove, relieved to rest her aching body.

Patricia looked over and snarled. "Don't get too comfortable, dearie. You've got work to do!"

Chapter Twenty-Nine:
Felicity

Inspector Rawlings stood at the bottom of the stairs leading to Terrance's flat. A young woman came out holding a baby in her arms. She looked over at the inspector as she settled the baby in a pram that stood outside her door. He pulled out his badge and held it up.

"Inspector Rawlings. Sussex Police."

She seemed indifferent to his badge.

"If you are looking for Terrence, he came by last night and left early this morning. I heard him running down the stairs. They make a hell of a racket, and I tell him all the time not to run because it wakes up the baby, but does he listen?"

She tutted, shaking her head. "What's he been up to now?"

Putting his badge in his pocket, he looked back up the stairs. "I just need to talk with him."

He tipped his hat and went up the stairs two at a time until he reached the top. He knocked on the door and waited.

"He leaves a key under the mat." She called up.

He looked down at her, a puzzled look making his frown. She shrugged. "I have to feed his cat."

Retrieving the key, he opened the front door. A ginger cat came rushing out past his feet and off down the stairs. He heard her calling the cat by its name as he went inside. The room was dour, and the smell of damp clung to the air. The wallpaper had peeled down from under the window, and a bare light bulb hung down

Secrets and Skeletons In The Teashop

from the ceiling. A solitary wooden table sat in the middle of the room with a screwed-up piece of paper on top. He walked over and unfurled the paper to read, "Eight o'clock — Spaniard."

After a few moments of studying it, he put it in his pocket. He searched each room, scouring around for any detail that stood out. In the bedroom, a stack of bird magazines was strewn across the floor. It wasn't a crime, but it helped link him to the egg smuggling, Patricia and Bill. He left frustrated, still no closer to finding out where Patricia had taken Faye.

Back at the station, he took out the note. He stared, wondering who the Spaniard was. Was Terrence meeting him somewhere? Maybe at the caves. He still didn't understand why Patricia had taken Faye. His back ached, and he leaned back in his chair, thinking. As the idea hit him, he jumped up, stuffing the note in the desk drawer. He passed the Desk Sergeant on his way out and said, "I'll be at Five Oaks Nursing Home if anyone needs to get a hold of me."

He saw the Sergeant jot it down as he left. He was taking a chance that Felicity would be on duty when he arrived at Five Oaks. His luck was in as he walked down the corridor. Penelope came out of a room carrying a tray of bandages and gauze. She froze as she saw him striding towards her.

"Hello, Felicity; I'd like a quick word, please."

"What's this!?" Mrs. Botley came rushing out of her office.

"Good afternoon, Mrs. Botley. I would like a quick word with Felicity."

Mrs. Botley stiffened her shoulders and looked away as if repelled by his words. "I thought this business had all been sorted."

"Not yet! I won't keep Felicity too long." She stood thinking longer than he was prepared to wait.

"Or I could take her down to the station with me. If it's inconvenient for you here."

"Well, I wouldn't want you to go to all that bother, inspector. You may use my office."

A tight-lipped smile swept across her face. He presumed it was the smile she used to greet unwelcome visitors. She stepped aside and took the tray off Penelope and walked off.

Inside the office, he shut the door.

"Please sit down Felicity. This won't take long."

Penelope, visibly nervous, brushed the sides of her skirt into place before sitting down. Her entire body language was closed. From her hands clasped together in her lap, to her legs neatly locked together, from the ankles to her knees. Her eyes were wide, like a scared mouse staring back at him. He smiled. A genuine smile, trying to put her at ease.

"I know we spoke briefly before." He deliberately avoided using Patricia's name. "But I must ask you again if you can tell me anything about the day of Jane Penny's death?"

She started hyperventilating and got up, running to the cupboard in the corner of the room. She pulled out a brown paper bag from the shelf and placed it over her mouth. Breathing in and out, inflating and then deflating the bag. After a few moments, she regained her composure and walked back over to her chair and sat down. He could see the colour had drained from her face, leaving her pale.

"Would you like me to fetch you a glass of water?"

She shook her head. "No, thank you." She took another breath in and out of the bag. Usually, he would leave the interview for a few hours, but he knew time was passing, and he needed to find Faye quickly.

"It is very important that you tell me everything, and I mean everything, that you know."

His eyes fixed on her bowed head as she looked at the paper bag she was holding in her lap. Still silent, she seemed unable to bring herself to speak. He raised his tone up a notch.

"You realise Patricia has abducted Miss Lantern and is on the run with her."

Jolted out of her silence, she looked up. "Why has she abducted Miss Lantern?"

"That's what I'm trying to establish. Can you tell me anything about the day Jane Penny was murdered?"

She gulped and took a deep breath in through her nose and out again.

"I saw Patricia coming out of Mrs. Penny's room around ten to eight."

He stared at her blankly. "Can you elaborate? Is there some significance to that?"

"We usually split the chores. I had only just helped Mrs. Penny to bed. Patricia was working the left side; I was working the right side of the corridor. We split the workload. She had no reason to be in Mrs. Penny's room."

She paused—"It was the same night Bill turned up."

"Does this Bill have a surname?"

Penny Townsend

"Bill Green."

He nodded. "What time did he turn up?"

"I'm not sure, but he was in the kitchen and Patricia came in and said I wasn't to say anything." She paused - a look of defiance in her eyes. "But I wrote Bill's name in the visitor's book."

He had suspected Penelope knew more about the torn page than she had let on and was grateful she had told him. It was hard evidence linking Bill and Patricia together at the crime scene.

"Thank you for telling me, Felicity; that is very helpful."

A smile tugged at her mouth, and he could see her shoulders relax.

"Can you tell me who discovered Mrs. Penny's body?"

Tears fell down her cheeks. "I did. I went to ask her if she wanted her usual cocoa."

"What time was this?"

She wiped a tear away with her hand.

"Just after Patricia came out of Mrs. Penny's room. Around six o'clock."

He picked up a pen lying on the desk and pulled a notebook from his pocket, furiously writing down notes and times.

"Can you tell me anything else?"

She shook her head silently.

He looked up from writing. "Does the name 'Spaniard' mean anything to you?"

Secrets and Skeletons In The Teashop

She shook her head. "No."

A knock on the door echoed out, swiftly followed by Mrs. Botley. "Inspector. Constable Pemberley is here to see you!" She stood with her hand on the door handle.

"Thank you, Mrs. Botley. We're finished here."

He turned to Felicity. "I need you to accompany me to the station to make a statement."

He walked out of the office and met Pemberley, rushing towards him.

"Sir! We may have a location for Miss Lantern."

His heart jumped as he heard the news.

"The lighthouse off the Bay by Grimmer Point."

"So, they got on a boat! Good work Pemberley!" His mind instantly realising why they couldn't find any footprints or traces of them before.

"Oh, it wasn't me. Gwen telephoned the station. She's with Daniel." Inspector Rawlings' face darkened as he locked eyes with him - Pemberley gulped.

"I think they have gone to the lighthouse!"

Chapter Thirty:
Sabotage

Patricia paced the floor, every now and then stopping to look out the kitchen window. Bill was sitting down at the table, checking the charts and maps.

"I think they'll take this route." He ran his finger along the map, tracing the route. Patricia looked over, uninterested.

"I'm going for a nap! Keep your eye on her."

She glanced over at Faye, who was sitting silently by the stove. She had nowhere to go. Bill had the keys to the boat. Satisfied, she went upstairs. Faye sat thinking about Inspector Rawlings and Daniel. It had been two days ago that she spoke to Daniel on the telephone and still no sign that anyone knew where she was. She watched Bill rolling up the charts. He walked over to a wooden dresser and pulled out the drawer.

"What does Patricia want me to do?"

He didn't look up, continuing to place the charts inside the drawer. "Nothing much. Just hand the eggs to the Spaniard."

"Who is the Spaniard?"

He slammed the drawer shut.

"It doesn't matter who he is. Just do what she asks." He hesitated, his brow furrowed, "and you'll be fine."

....
....

Daniel was still throwing up as another boat came into view.

Secrets and Skeletons In The Teashop

"Whose boat is that?" he said, retching over the side again as Olly pulled alongside the wooden jetty. Gwen jumped off and grabbed the rope, mooring them next to the small fishing boat. Her eye caught the name on its white hull— the 'Sea Salter.' She had seen it before, moored in Olly's yard.

"It's Bill's," she said. And jumped on board the fishing boat.

"For the love of God, Gwen." Daniel jumped onto the jetty with Buster. "Someone could be inside," his voice lost in the noise of an enormous wave crashing against the rocks.

Gwen tried the cabin handle, pulling it down as Daniel caught up and stood on the jetty.

"It's locked! They'll be at the lighthouse. We need to hurry."

Daniel looked around nervously.

"We are picking the wrong fight here, Gwen!" His voice was now anxious. She leaped back onto the jetty and looked blankly at him before glancing up at the path toward the lighthouse.

"What are you talking about?"

Wide-eyed with fear, he said, "They have a gun!"

She turned and looked sharply at him.

"And how do you think Faye feels right now? Would you rather leave her imprisoned in there with those crazy people and do nothing?!"

Anger and guilt twisted his stomach into a knot as he thought about Faye.

"Well, I sure as hell know charging in like Ringo Kid and Wonder Woman isn't going to help her!"

With a defiant snort, she folded her arms across her chest and looked away.

"Look. You called Inspector Rawlings — he will be on his way." His expression suddenly changed. "You called him, didn't you?"

Gwen sighed and shook her head. Accepting that as a yes, he continued.

"Why can't we just wait like normal people?" He threw his hands in the air in disbelief.

"You would never have got on a boat to the lighthouse in the first place!"

Then he panicked as Gwen walked away. "Where are you going?"

Buster pulled on the lead, whipping it out of his hand, and shot past them.

"Buster! For pity's sake. Buster! That's all I need!"

Gwen took off after Buster, and Daniel ran on the spot for a few steps in a panic before his brain finally gave in and ran after them. Watching the scene unfold as they ran by, Olley called out, "I'll stay here and watch the boat!"

Daniel thought that was the only sensible thing he had heard all day, as the boat was the only way back and salvation from the hideous nightmare of a day he was having!

As he ran up the stone path, the lighthouse's looming presence stood tall above him. He heard Buster barking and saw Gwen running to pick up his lead. He froze as Bill Green appeared at the kitchen window. A few seconds later, the door opened, and Bill

Secrets and Skeletons In The Teashop

stood face to face with Gwen, gun in hand. Buster ran past his legs and into the lighthouse as Bill waved his gun at Gwen, motioning for her to go inside. Daniel gasped and turned to sit with his back against the rock. His eyes searched the sea for any signs of Inspector Rawlings and a boat full of gun-toting police officers approaching, but the only thing he could see was gathering storm clouds ahead as the sky turned a thunderous grey.

....
....

Faye burst into tears at the sight of Buster running towards her, closely followed by Gwen as she ran forward and threw herself at Faye, hugging her tightly.

"Faye. You're okay!"

Their reunion was short-lived, as a loud explosion outside made Faye jump.

Bill rushed to the kitchen window again. "What now?"

A few moments later, he shouted up the stairs, "Patricia!"

As she came charging down the stairs, he handed her his gun and raced out the door.

....
....

Olly was checking the radio inside the cabin and didn't notice a small boat pull around the Bay and slip into the Cove out of sight.

Terrance moored up, jumping from his boat onto the rocks. He'd done it many times before, acting as the go-between for Patricia, who always wanted to stay in the background, out of sight.

Penny Townsend

He had saved just enough money to disappear and start a new life outside the village, and this was his last opportunity for some big money and Patricia wasn't going to get away with pushing him out. He would have his vengeance on her for, as he suspected, killing his mother. Now, she and Bill would pay.

He made his way over the rocks with only a small climb around the bottom of the jagged cliff face until he was in line with the two boats moored on the jetty. He could see Bill's fishing boat, but he didn't recognise the other boat. It wasn't the Spaniard who always moored on the other side of the island. A figure moving about in the cabin caught his eye, and he recognised Olly in his distinctive hat. He had repaired his boat a few years ago.

Unnoticed, he slipped down the bank and behind Bill's boat, climbing quietly onboard. Moving to the stern of the boat, he lifted the hatch and crouched down, retrieving a metal fuel can. Opening the lid, he splashed it around the deck and up to the cabin until the can was empty. He laid the can down on the deck and looked around. Olly was still in the cabin of his own boat as he slid over the rails and back onto the jetty. He pulled a box of matches from his pocket and struck one, throwing it onto the deck. The deck ignited in an explosive bang that sent him reeling backward to the floor as orange flames took hold, rapidly spreading along the deck and engulfing the cabin.

Thick black smoke billowed up into the sky as he scrambled to his feet and ran back along the cliff face. He smiled to himself. Patricia had no way back except the other boat. He stopped and looked back. Olly was on the jetty, undoing the ropes that moored Bill's boat, letting it drift loose so the flames would not spread to his own boat.

At a swift pace, he made his way around the cliff, taking the uneven south-facing path along to the lighthouse. He needed to know who Olly was waiting for. He crouched down behind a large boulder and saw a man visibly shaking, sitting behind a rock. Beyond him, the door to the lighthouse opened, and Bill came rushing out, heading for the jetty. He could see Patricia looking out the far window of the lighthouse; his body tensed, and anger flashed across his eyes. This was his opportunity to retrieve the eggs. Vengeance in his step, he sprinted down the gravel track, slipping as he reached the bottom and rushed into the lighthouse, locking the door behind him.

Penny Townsend

Chapter Thirty-One:
One Step Behind

Inspector Rawlings walked down the beach. His men were each handed a life jacket as they stepped on board. Already briefed, they sat on the boat, looking out in silence. Pemberley and two other officers hung over the side, retching as the boat lifted and dropped with the waves.

Black storm clouds were gathering overhead as they approached the Bay and Inspector Rawlings clung to the sides as they turned to see a boat engulfed in flames, black smoke filling the air above them as it drifted out to sea. He watched the captain grab the radio handset and send out a mayday- another boat in the area would tow it to shore.

Pulling up at the jetty, his men jumped off, guns pulled, aimed at the other boat moored up. Olly came out with his hands up as Inspector Rawlings approached him.

"Olly! What are you doing here?"

Olly lowered his hands and shook his head. He put one hand on his heart and, in a strong Jamaican accent, said, "Man. Me relieved to see you, inspector. There's some crazy stuff happening here! Me here with Gwen on a rescue mission to help her friend Faye."

His heart missed a beat as he heard Faye's name, and a glimmer of hope danced in his eyes before annoyance at Gwen for getting herself involved ran through his mind. He went to question Olly when Bill Green suddenly appeared, running down the path. He skidded to a stop in shock as he saw them all standing there and turned tail, running back up the path.

"After him!" He called out as his men scrambled into action and gave chase. He turned back to Olly.

Secrets and Skeletons In The Teashop

"Where is Gwen now?"

"She went off with Daniel to the lighthouse."

"Daniel's here too!?"

Olly nodded and pointed up the path. "Up that way. Me keeping an eye on me boat." He looked in the direction that Bill's boat had drifted out of the Bay. "Some crazy person set light to the other fishing boat that was moored up next to mine."

"Did you see what happened?"

"Me only saw a man running back up behind the cliff after the explosion."

He nodded. "Stay here. If Gwen comes back, keep her here with you."

Olly raised his hand in a small salute to him, inclining his head.

"Will do."

He took off up the path. None of his men were in sight as he reached the large boulder that flanked the lighthouse. His eyes strained to look through the windows for signs of movement inside, but everything was still. A sudden movement caught his eye. Daniel stood up and was about to run towards the lighthouse.

"Daniel!" he shouted as he ducked down and headed towards him.

Daniel staggered back and gasped.

"Oh, thank the Lord! Inspector! Gwen is trapped inside the lighthouse. I saw Patricia and Bill and a gun! I was about to go in."

Inspector Rawlings held up his hand to Daniel, who was now hyperventilating.

"Relax, Daniel. I'll take it from here."

His face was stern as he surveyed the lighthouse and surrounding area. "Who else is inside the lighthouse?"

Wide-eyed, Daniel blurted out, "Buster. He ran straight in."

Inspector Rawlings clenched his jaw. "What about Faye?"

"Buster dragged us here and ran inside. That means Faye must be in the lighthouse, too."

He turned to scan the lighthouse again. He could feel the adrenaline pumping through his body as his eyes searched for movement along the kitchen window.

"Wait here. I'm going down to see who's inside. If my men arrive, tell them where I am."

....
....

Terrance moved quietly around the lighthouse. Looking around the room where Patricia had been standing. The stove had been lit, but it was as though nobody had been there. He made his way upstairs. Pushing the bedroom door open, he walked to the window. Down below, running across the island, he could see Patricia with a gun on Faye and Gwen, pushing them forward into the Cove. He watched them disappear through the trees, followed by Faye's dog. He rushed back downstairs and followed them out through the lighthouse door. Patricia was leading them to the far side of the island to meet the Spaniard - but he was about to change all that and sped up.

Chapter Thirty-Two:
The Spaniard

Inspector Rawlings ran down to the lighthouse and stood with his back against the wall. He turned his head sideways to look in through the window. His eyes scanned the room. There was no one about. He turned the handle of the lighthouse door, but someone had locked it from the inside. He made his way around the white curved wall, ducking under the window, and reached the rear entrance. The door was wide open. He could see through the gap in into the empty room. There were no telltale voices carrying out. No noise at all. He made his way inside, his eyes searching for any clue.

Pemberley came rushing through the door, followed by two armed officers. He motioned for them to check upstairs as another officer pushed a handcuffed Bill Green into the room. He looked tired. His head bowed as though all the fight had gone out of him. Inspector Rawling's eyes narrowed as he looked at him.

"Where are Faye and Gwen?"

"With Patricia."

Inspector Rawling's body tensed. "Where is Patricia now?"

"She's on her way to meet the Spaniard on the far side of the island at Gull Cove." Bill looked over to the open back door. He inclined his head forward.

"Straight out the door and down the Cove. Then turn West at Dead Man's Rock. It's a giant boulder. You can't miss it."

Inspector Rawlings nodded at the officer holding Bill.

"Take him to the boat. And there is a man, Daniel, who needs some help. He's outside at the top of the path. Take him with you and look after him."

He turned to Pemberley and the other two officers.

"You three. With me!"

He set off running down towards the Cove with the officers close behind him, desperate to reach Faye and Gwen.

....
....

Patricia looked down the steep descent to Gull Cove below. She could see the Spaniard's blue and white boat moored out from the rocks. The sail was lowered, and it bobbed majestically with the waves, tipping back and forth. It took what seemed like an age to descend the steps until they finally reached the sand below. Patricia kept the gun pointed at Gwen whilst she spoke to Faye.

"This is a simple exchange. Take the box and give it to the man on the deck of the Spaniard. He'll give you a rucksack. If he asks where Terrance is, just tell him he's sick, and you're his girlfriend, come in his place." Her eyes bore through her as she said.

"And don't be pulling any funny business. Your friend is still here."

Faye could see the terrified look on Gwen's face as Patricia pointed the gun at her. Buster leaned his head into her leg as if sensing her fear. With a trembling hand, she reached down and reassured him.

"It's okay, Buster. Wait here."

She took the box and started walking towards the boat. Shaking, she looked back as Patricia called out, "Don't be handin' the box over until you have the rucksack in your hand."

Secrets and Skeletons In The Teashop

She pushed the gun nearer to Gwen's head, and Faye turned away, sick to her stomach. As she approached the boat, a wiry, tanned man with dark hair and even darker brown eyes glared at her. He placed one hand on the side of the boat and jumped over into the water up to his waist. With a rucksack slung over one shoulder, he waded his way forward, meeting her at the edge of the sea as it lapped the shore. He looked behind her, his eyes scanning the rocks and caves.

Shaking, she held her ground. "I'm here in place of my boyfriend. He's too sick to come."

He looked back at her, his eyes filled with mistrust from years of experience of any change in people or circumstances.

"I have the eggs." She held out the box in front of him.

He glanced at her and went to take it as she pulled it back. Patricia pointed the gun at Gwen's head in her mind. She held out her other hand.

"The rucksack!"

He glared at her, his eyes hard and fixed. She held her breath, then let out a sigh of relief as his muscular arm swung the rucksack off his shoulder and held it out. She took it and handed him the box. Lifting the lid, his mouth parted into a smile. He turned around and quickly splashed back through the waves. Another man on deck, who had watched the entire event, leaned an arm down and helped him up onto the Spaniard. She turned around and walked back, breathing heavily until she reached Patricia, who snatched the rucksack from her and barked,

"Sit down over there!"

Wearily, she dropped onto the sand. Buster came and sat down with her, gently nudging her with his nose. Patricia untied the rucksack and a sickly smile crept along her lips. Gwen was sitting near Patricia and her heart missed a beat as Gwen jumped up and rushed her, pouncing on her from behind. Patricia swung around, sending her off balance to the floor. Faye sprung up and covered Gwen with her arms and body and screamed.

"No!"

Patricia held the gun towards her, the tic under her eye quivering. Buster barked as Faye closed her eyes tightly, waiting as Patricia stood with her arm out, pointing the gun at them. The Spaniard's white sails catching the wind as it sailed out of the cove caught Patricia's eye. The sound of a gunshot would alert them and potentially create a witness. She dropped her hand and moved around them; anger laced her voice as she spat. "Sit with your backs together."

Faye moved around and sat behind Gwen as Patricia pulled at the rope tying the rucksack. She made a noose and wrapped it around both their hands, pulling it tight behind their backs. She smiled and straightened up. Gulls calling out, circling as storm clouds engulfed the skies, drew Faye's attention up. Her eyes dropped to see the back of Patricia, already halfway across the sand, heading out of the cove.

"Are you okay, Gwen?"

Gwen was silent for a moment.

"Why is she leaving us here?"

Faye watched Patricia struggle to get a foothold before finally climbing up the large boulder and back up the hill with the rucksack. She pulled at the rope digging into her wrist.

"It gives her time to get away before we get free. Can you reach the knot with your fingers?"

Gwen winced in pain as the rope cut into her hand.

Secrets and Skeletons In The Teashop

"It's no good. I can't budge it. Oh, my God, Faye! The water!"

Faye looked down to see the waves were coming in fast, only a few feet away from them.

"Can you stand up?"

After several attempts, they realised it was impossible. Patricia had tied the ropes so tight they couldn't move. As they tried to push up with their feet, the wet sand shifted from under them. Tears fell down Gwen's face as the cold seawater lapped over their outstretched legs. Faye pulled harder at her wrist and winced as pain sheared up her arm. Buster barked and suddenly took off, jumping up on the rocks and up the hill. At least he will be safe, she thought as she watched him disappear.

Gwen became hysterical, screaming and writhing about, pulling them to one side. Faye dug her heels into the sand, battling to hold them upright, and screamed at her.

"Stop, Gwen! You're making it worse!"

Her eyes fell on the massive boulder in front of her. The mossy green line that marked the high tide was above her head. The water reached their elbows, and Gwen's voice was frantic.

"I should have listened to Daniel!"

Faye's mind was on Tom and how she desperately wanted to see him. Her eyes searched the cliff tops, hoping he would magically appear. The tide had swelled up to their shoulders, and Gwen screamed at the top of her voice.

"I don't want to die like this! I can't! I just can't!"

Faye had no reply. She realized all the years she had spent waiting for Tommy had been wasted. Now, it was too late. The tide moved their bodies, lifting them up, and Gwen screamed in terror, frantically digging her feet into the sand. The tide was lapping at their necks, the cold water making her shiver. She could feel herself slipping sideways as an enormous wave crashed over them. She grabbed Gwen's hand as they went under, her feet trying to gain purchase in the sand as they rolled under the water. Any noise from the gulls was now gone as the sea echoed out around them.

Pain ripped through her arm as Gwen's body jolted, kicking and tugging at their hands. As the water receded, she felt waves pouring over her back as she rose to the surface, dragged up by an unseen force. Gasping for air, she saw Terrance standing over them, his face strained.

His taut arms dragged and pulled them towards the rocks. Buster stood barking on the cliff edge as she spluttered and coughed out seawater. Terrance pulled a penknife from his pocket and swiftly cut the rope, binding them together. Faye desperately clung to the boulder as he climbed up, pulling Gwen to him first. Faye's fingers slipped on the rock face, and terror filled her body as she gasped and disappeared under the water. She felt a hand grab her arm as Terrance dragged her to him, pulling her back up and out of the water. Rocks spiraling and tumbling down the path hit the boulder they were laying on as Inspector Rawlings and his men came rushing down the hill. Terrance jumped off the boulder and dived into the water. Reaching the other side, he climbed out. Seeing the officers draw their guns, Inspector Rawlings cried out.

"Hold your fire!"

He knelt down between Faye and Gwen. Gwen, still spluttering, sat up. He put his arm under Faye and helped her sit up. Relief surged through his veins. Her heart leaped at the sight of him. The feel of his arms around her made her turn her head closer to him. Finding relief in the warmth of his body, she murmured,

"Tom."

Pemberley rushed forward as he held her tighter. "Shall we give chase, sir?"

He stared at Terrance as he took off, climbing up the rocks and across the track. He would be forever grateful to him. Glad to have Faye safe in his arms, he lifted her up.

"No. Give me a hand to get Faye and Gwen safely back up the hill." For the first time in his life, he let a known criminal escape.

Chapter Thirty-Three:
Race Against Time

Patricia left the cove running and took the long track that led around the main path. Sometimes, the local Harbour took sightseers around the island, and she didn't want anyone to see her leave the bay. As she rounded the bend, she heard the pounding of footsteps running along the main path. She ducked down behind a crumbling wall that connected to the lighthouse garden. Her mouth formed into a sneer as she saw Inspector Rawlings and his men running past. She needed to find Bill quickly and set off again. As she reached the lighthouse, she could see a police officer walking around outside and waited until he turned the corner before slinking around the back. She reached the cliffs overlooking the jetty and, ducking low, laid down on the grass, her eyes scouring the jetty.

Bill was nowhere in sight; neither was his boat. For an instant, she wondered if he had seen the police and left the island and her behind. Her fingers clasped tightly around the rucksack. He wouldn't be getting his hands on any of the money.

In the distance, a fishing boat moored behind the police boat bobbed up and down. A man just visible in the cabin caught her eye. She made her way down behind the cliff and stopped, smiling to herself. Coming into view was the tourist boat loaded with eager people waiting to see the lighthouse and island.

The wind was picking up, rushing through the bay, tipping the boat, rocking it sideways. The Captain was taking a risk bringing tourists to the island with an approaching storm, but it was nearing the end of the tourist season, and he wasn't going to lose any money.

Patricia could hear the shouts as the police officer frantically waved his arms at the captain, telling him to turn around. The man in the other boat jumped off and joined the officer, who was now arguing with the protesting captain. A young lad jumped off the tourist boat onto the jetty and moored them in front of the police boat.

She wouldn't have long. Just enough time to get down to the boat and get away. Her pace quickened as she started making her way down the track when she heard a noise behind her.

She turned to see Terrance; his eyes fixed on her. Shocked, she knew she couldn't outrun him and swiftly pulled the rucksack up, frantically reaching inside for the gun. She felt a sting of pain shear across her fingers as Terrance ripped the bag from her hand, making her stumble forward. He stood over her, anger in his voice.

"Not this time! You aren't getting away with it this time!"

He reached into the bag and grabbed the gun — she gasped, watching as his finger slowly squeezed the trigger, his eyes fixed on her. A voice behind him carried from the top of the hill, shouting his name.

"Terrance!"

Inspector Rawlings could see him standing with the gun pointed at Patricia. He shouted again as he ran down the hill, slowing as he reached them.

"Terrance! Put the gun down."

Terrance's eyes were full of rage. He was hoping one wrong move from Patricia turning to run would make it easy. But she stood frozen in fear.

Inspector Rawlings raised his hands cautiously as he reached them.

"Terrence, please. Let me deal with this."

"Why should I? She killed my father and my mother." His eyes narrowed on Patricia as he pointed the gun at her.

Slowly, he edged closer to him. His voice was calm.

"Because you're not like her. You're not a killer."

After a few moments, which felt like an eternity to Patricia, he lowered the gun. Inspector Rawlings reached down and slowly took the gun from his shaking hand as his men came running down the track. The wind was now racing along the island. Thunder boomed out like a cannon blast, and lightning flashed across the sea, lighting up the boats.

"Into the lighthouse!" He called back as the rain started hammering down. They ran the last few hundred yards, reaching the back of the lighthouse. The door swung open, banging against the wall as they ran in. After fighting the wind to close it behind them, his eyes searched the room. He sighed with relief. Faye was safe, sitting on the sofa by the stove.

Pemberley ran over to the window. Through the torrent of rain, he could just make out figures running up the path. He could tell some of them were fellow officers and ran over to the front door to unbolt it. Opening the door, he braced himself against the wind and rain blasting in. An officer ran inside, followed by Daniel, then another officer with Bill Green still in handcuffs. Inspector Rawlings stared in shock as a group of people drenched to the skin came piling through the door, followed by Olly and another man wearing a captain's hat. As Pemberley shut the door, the noise of the terrified tourists was deafening. He held up his hands,

"Quiet. Quiet, please!" As they all stopped to look at him, he turned to the officer standing near him.

"Turner, what's going on here?"

Turner threw his hands up.

Secrets and Skeletons In The Teashop

"I tried turning the captain away, but they moored up and jumped off before I could stop them."

Cameras hanging around their necks and oversized hats and beach bags made it easy to see they were tourists. He raised his voice again.

"I'm Inspector Rawlings, Sussex police. And these are my men."

He pointed out his officers by name until he reached Pemberley.

"If you have any concerns, speak to Officer Pemberley… But —" He stressed, "I need to make sure you all stay here together until the storm has passed."

A man in shorts and a tee shirt, wet through, shouted, "Why are the police here? What's going on?" His eyes were briefly directed towards Bill's handcuffs. "Are we in any danger?"

There were a few nods and affirmations from the other tourists, all of them staring at the inspector, anxiously waiting for a response.

"There's nothing to be alarmed about. We've had a minor incident, which has been taken care of."

He glanced at Patricia, who was being restrained by one of the officers.

"You can all relax and make yourselves comfortable until the storm passes."

"What are we supposed to do while we are waiting?" another woman piped up. He nodded to Pemberley.

"Please address any concerns you may have to Officer Pemberley."

As they disbanded, talking amongst themselves, he sighed with relief and turned to Officer Turner.

"Get Bill and Patricia upstairs out of sight and keep them apart."

He posted another officer at the foot of the stairs to stop anyone from venturing near and moved Terrance into the opposite room and shut the door, locking him in.

He looked over to see Faye sitting on the sofa, her head back, resting. He wanted to go over to her. To hold her and reassure her. But circumstances dictated he kept fully focused on what potentially was a highly volatile situation, having members of the public confined in the lighthouse with criminals.

He looked out the window. Lightning flashed twice as the storm took hold and he wondered how the men and women who worked the lighthouse years ago must have felt in these conditions. He looked back at Faye again, his heart set on letting her know his true feelings. He would not make the mistake of letting her slip away from him.

Chapter Thirty-Four:
The Storm

Faye looked around the room. Gwen was sitting next to her on the sofa, unusually quiet and pale. She wanted to hold it together for her sake, but inside, she was still shaking. Facing death had shocked her to her core. Daniel had made his way through the throng of tourists milling about, picking up lanterns and books, posing to take pictures with them.

"Aunty Faye. You had us worried."

Faye looked down to see the sofa had soaked up the sea water from her clothes, turning it a darker shade of green.

"Oh Daniel, I thought Gwen and I…... were…."

She looked over to see Inspector Rawlings talking with one of his men. Lightning flashed outside, silhouetting the side of his face, framing it against the window. The line of his face strong. He turned as if sensing her gaze upon him. His eyebrow raised up over his left eye, and his head lifted slightly up and down as if asking if she was okay. Drawn to him, the corners of her mouth curved into a smile, almost as if she couldn't stop them if she wanted to. She nodded back, and he reciprocated; a flash of longing momentarily seemed to hold his eyes on her before he turned back. She felt Buster nudge her, breaking her gaze, as he laid his head on her lap.

"It was Buster who went and got help," Daniel said as he sat on the arm of the sofa next to Gwen, making Faye turn back to him.

"Really?"

"Yes. We heard him barking and then we saw him at the cliff top, disappearing over the edge with Terrance in tow as we were running down the path."

She stroked Buster's head again. "What would I do without you?" She whispered as he laid down, contented, at her feet. Daniel nudged Gwen gently with his arm.

"So, how's Wonder Woman?"

Gwen's mouth pulled back in one corner. "I'm still here, aren't I?"

He smirked. "Well, it wasn't for the lack of trying to get yourself killed!"

"Daniel!" Faye snapped. "Gwen's been through enough without you adding to it."

He raised his hands. "You're right. I'm sorry." He looked at Gwen with compassion in his eyes. "I'm just glad you and Aunty Faye are safe, and we can put this whole sordid business behind us."

Gwen nodded silently.

Faye looked at the locked door which Terrance was behind. She wanted to thank him for saving her life but now wasn't the right time.

"Terrance is locked up, and Patricia and Bill are being held safely upstairs. I think we can relax."

Daniel turned abruptly to her.

"I'm not relaxing just yet. Not until..."

A loud crash from upstairs made everyone look up. Daniel clasped his hands on his head. "Oh, no. Not again."

Inspector Rawlings raced up the stairs to several gasps from the tourists.

Secrets and Skeletons In The Teashop

"It's nothing to worry about!" Daniel said, jumping up. "Inspector Rawlings has it under control."

Faye saw him cross his fingers behind his back.

"Let's all just stay calm!"

Chapter Thirty-Five:
Nowhere to Run

His heart pounding, Inspector Rawlings rushed up the stairs, followed by the officer stationed outside Terrance's room and Pemberley. As they burst through the door, Bill Green was grappling with Turner, his hands dripping with blood as he held a long shard of glass between his cuffed hands. He lunged at Turner, cutting across the top of his forearm. Patricia was in the corner of the room, sitting on a chair, silent as Turner recoiled in pain. The other officers rushed Bill, pinning him to the ground, when Inspector Rawlings felt a tug on the back of his belt, and his stomach dropped in realization - Patricia had grabbed the gun from behind his jacket. She stood wild-eyed, pointing it towards them as they stood up and raised their arms. Turner and Bill were still on the floor as she edged out the door, taking the key.

Bill called out as he struggled to stand up, "Patricia! Wait!"

But she locked the door behind him and crept down the stairs, concealing the gun behind her. She made her way through a group of tourists standing at the bottom and headed for the door, when a woman screamed.

"She has a gun!"

Panic ensued as screams rang out, and people bumped into each other in the confusion. The doorway was now blocked by people running in chaos. A man approached her, and she pulled her arm from behind her back, pointing the gun at him. As more screams erupted, he backed away, and she saw Faye on the sofa. A tic pulled under her eye as her lip curled up into a snarl.

"Get up!"

Secrets and Skeletons In The Teashop

Faye could hardly believe Patricia was standing there pointing a gun at her again. She stared, terrified, as Patricia shouted,

"Move!"

She grabbed Faye by the arm as she stood up, pushing the gun into her back, edging out the room as everyone parted to let her pass. Opening the door, the storm blasted rain into the doorway, nearly knocking them over. Bracing herself against the wind, she turned.

"If anyone follows us," her eyes quickly glanced to Gwen and Daniel as she lifted the gun to Faye's head. "She's dead," and a gasp rang out as she pushed Faye out into the howling wind.

Another crash upstairs, as Pemberley put his shoulder on the door to break it down, was followed by Pemberley and Inspector Rawlings thundering down the stairs. Running through the crowd of people, his eyes searching for Faye on the empty sofa. He cast his eyes around the room, fear knotting his stomach. Daniel came rushing up, his arms flaying wildly in a panic.

"Patricia has taken Faye. She had a gun at her head as they went outside." He pointed to the front door of the Lighthouse.

With his worst fears realized and dread filling every fiber of his body, he ran out the lighthouse door, head down, into the raging storm.

....
....

Patricia had nowhere to go on the island and could only leave by boat. But surely, she wouldn't get on the boat in this storm. The wind pushed him backward, howling as it slowed his pace until he finally reached the jetty. His heart stopped as he saw Patricia trying to start the engine on the boat. Faye clung to the side as a spark of lightning flashed across the sky, followed by a surge of water, tipping the boat sideways. Patricia fell forward and then back, the gun she was holding flew from her hand as she grabbed the sides. Faye dropped to her knees, holding on as another wave pushed the boat up, throwing Patricia forward. She stumbled and fell on top of the gun. She snatched it up, put it back into her pocket, and stood up. A man's voice called out, making her turn.

"Faye!"

Patricia shot a glance over in his direction. Trying to steady herself as the boat rocked and dipped violently into another surge of waves. She pulled the gun from her pocket and aimed at him.

Faye screamed and jumped to her feet. She lunged at Patricia, sending the gun flying up into the air as the noise of the shot rang out. Patricia shoved her to the floor of the boat as the gun landed in the water.

"You are interfering." She went to grab Faye when another wave surged forward, tipping the boat up in the air and throwing her back and overboard into the crashing waves. Faye gasped, horrified, as she watched Patricia disappear under the water.

Running down to the boat, Inspector Rawlings jumped on. Grabbing hold of the side, he called out to Faye. The noise of the rain was so loud that his voice was barely audible. Deafening thunder clapped out above her head as she held onto the middle seat, moving around the boat as he edged towards her in rhythm with the boat as it dipped and swayed. Reaching out, he grabbed her outstretched hand and pulled her to him, holding her tightly with one arm while the other clung to the boat, watching as Pemberley and Turner hurried towards them from the jetty.

He shouted to be heard over the wind and rain lashing down.

"Get Faye back to the lighthouse!"

Secrets and Skeletons In The Teashop

He looked back into the sea. The waves were crashing in, and it was impossible to see anything in the water. It would be a miracle if Patricia survived.

Chapter Thirty-Six:
Gone

The storm raged outside as Faye battled her way through the violent gusts of wind that almost took her off her feet. With her head down against the rain, she ran to the safety of the lighthouse with Pemberley and Turner. It would be a few hours before the storm died down enough to get back on the boat.

Leaning his shoulder into the door, Pemberley pushed it open. Faye walked into gasps and spontaneous applause from the tourists. Just seeing her unharmed was a relief to all of them. Embarrassed, she smiled and made her way quickly over to the desk by the window. Daniel rushed over to her with Gwen, and they both threw their arms around her in unbridled happiness. Daniel stood back, taking on a serious tone,

"Aunty Faye! I'm not sure I can handle any more escapades with criminals! It's exhausting!"

Gwen let out a laugh. The color was now back in her cheeks as she hugged Faye again.

"She's safe and well and back with us, and that's all that matters."

Faye put her arm around Gwen.

"Thank you. It means a lot to me that you both care so much."

She glanced up to see Inspector Rawlings looking over at her. Guilt nagging at her, she smiled and looked away. She was waiting for Tommy to come back. She had made a promise to him. But now, as she looked back at Inspector Rawlings, she could feel her heart stirring. She knew she was falling in love with him.

Secrets and Skeletons In The Teashop

....
....

Inspector Rawlings walked into the room where Terrance was being held, followed by Pemberley, who marched Bill Green into the room, handcuffs still on but sporting a bandage wrapped around the cut on his hand. He waited until they were all settled in the room and turned to face Bill and Terrance. His face strained, and he looked away momentarily. He didn't like to see anyone come to harm as Patricia did. He looked back at them and cleared his throat.

"I thought you should both know Patricia attempted to escape the island by boat, but unfortunately, the storm tipped the boat, and she was thrown overboard."

"We have to presume she drowned." He said solemnly.

Bill gasped in horror.

Terrance sneered. "Good riddance to her!"

Bill flew at him, but Terrance was too quick and side-stepped, mocking him.

"You're a fool! Why would you care about her? She has done nothing but drag you into her mess."

A fire now burned in Terrance's eyes as he turned to Inspector Rawlings.

"Patricia killed my father!"

Bill shouted at him. "Shut up, Terrance!"

"And Bill and me, we carried his body to the tea shop and put it in the wall."

Penny Townsend

Inspector Rawlings pursed his lips, his face serious as he looked first at Terrance.

"Terrance Penny and William Green, I'm arresting you both as accomplices to the murder of Wilfred Penny."

Bill flew at Terrance again, but Pemberley moved his body to block him, grabbing his arms and holding him back.

Terrance shrugged. "It's over. I'm not hiding any longer."

Turner came through the door, his forearm covered in a bandage. He glanced at Bill as he walked up to Inspector Rawlings.

"We have everyone down at the boats, and we are all set to go."

Relieved, his mind drifted to Faye and getting her back to safety.

"Right. Let's get a move on Pemberley." He strode to the door, following Turner out of the room. As they approached the front door, Terrance stopped.

"Inspector! I need the lav. You've had me cooped up in that room for hours. I can't go on the boat without going to the lav first!"

Terence stared unblinking at him, his hands pulled in close to his body, making it clear he wasn't moving another inch without causing trouble.

Inspector Rawlings sighed. He wanted to get off the island as quickly as possible and this would be another delay.

"Alright, Terrance. Pemberley. Go with Terrance. Turner. you come with me."

He grabbed Bill by the arm and ushered him outside, hurrying down the path to the waiting boats. Their lights shone out, lighting

Secrets and Skeletons In The Teashop

up the jetty as the tourists noisily chatted. He glanced over, and his heart jumped as he saw Faye smiling at him. He turned back to Bill—he needed to focus.

"In the boat, Bill."

He got on the boat and positioned Bill between himself and Turner, making him sit on the boat floor. He wasn't risking losing him over the side. After five minutes had passed, he stood up.

"Where the hell has Pemberley got to?"

He saw a shadow move in the distance as he peered into the darkness. Pemberley suddenly appeared, running down the path, shouting.

"He's escaped! Terrance has escaped!"

The tourists, like startled geese, broke into noisy chattering as Inspector Rawlings asked.

"How?"

Pemberley swallowed nervously. "He climbed out the toilet window."

He couldn't tell whether Pemberley's face was red from running or from feeling embarrassed at a rookie mistake of not checking there was a window his prisoner could escape out of before he let him enter the toilet. He looked out across the island. It would be impossible to find him now in the pitch-black. Terrance knew the island well and probably had planned out several boat holes to run to if anything had gone wrong with his dealings with the Spaniard.

"Get on, Pemberley! We'll deal with him tomorrow."

As the boat engine started, Terrence watched, crouched down behind the large boulder near the lighthouse. Good! They were leaving. He watched the light of the boats fade in the distance and ran back into the lighthouse. Taking the lantern from the shelf, he lit the candle and made his way out through the back door, walking back down the track. He stopped. Retracing his footsteps from his earlier encounter with Patricia. His eyes searched the tall tufts of grass scattered around. A smile crept across his mouth as he sprinted a few feet, picking up the rucksack that he had thrown out of Patricia's reach.

In all the commotion with the gun, the inspector hadn't seen the bag lying in the dirt. Opening it up, he checked inside to see the bundles of notes still intact. He swung the bag over his shoulder and headed to the cove where his boat was moored. Today had worked out better than he could have hoped for. Patricia was gone. Bill was in custody, and he had all the money. All he needed now was for his boat to have survived the storm.

Chapter Thirty-Seven:
Done For

Faye relaxed in the back of the police car with Gwen, Daniel, and Buster who sat at her feet. Relief flooded over her as they pulled up at The Station House in the early hours of the morning. Gwen hugged her as she got out of the car.

"I'll see you tomorrow." With a tired wave goodbye, she walked across the road to the bakery as Daniel shut the Station House door behind them.

"You know we'll be the talk of the village tomorrow. Bonnie and Clyde will have nothing on me and Gwen." He sighed.

Faye was too tired to care. She walked up the stairs and into her room, collapsing onto the bed. As Buster trotted behind and curled up in his basket, Faye had already passed out from exhaustion.

....
....

Terrance could just make out the outline of his boat in the moonlight. Washed up on the shore, the sharp line of its resting hull catching his eye. He looked back at the water's edge. The noise of the waves washing ashore surrounded him, but the tide was out. In a few hours, it would come back in and right the boat. He would have to wait. It wasn't ideal, but he could sail at first light before the undoubted return of Inspector Rawlings and his men. He walked down the beach, pebbles crunching underfoot, as he found an alcove set back into the cliff face and sat down, closing his eyes. Rest would fall easily to him.

....

Penny Townsend

The sun coming up on the horizon glinted across the ripples of water. Terrance stirred as a large Herring Gull calling out to its mate made him jump awake with a start. Opening his eyes, he looked around and scanned the horizon. Where was his boat? He looked down. And the money? After frantically searching the surrounding sand, he jumped to his feet. The tide was in, but not enough to reach where the money had been lying next to him. His heart missed a beat. Surely Patricia couldn't have survived the storm? He charged up the rocks, his feet slipping in his haste to climb to the top of the cliff. Standing on the highest point, he shaded his eyes, looking out across the sea with his hand.

He could see a boat in the Bay, tearing through the water as its white wake followed behind it. But the boat was coming towards the island, not away from it. As it neared, he saw it suddenly turn sharply and head off behind the cliff that jutted out, masking the other side of the island. He ran as fast as his legs would carry him down to the track and then up, racing across to the other side of the island. He stopped on the top of the south-facing cliff to see Inspector Rawlings and his men speeding along, slamming into waves as they went flat out to catch another boat. It was his boat! And Patricia was driving it! Anger flared up in him. This was the last time she messed with him. She was heading for the safety of the cove as he tore off back down the cliff.

....
....

Patricia cursed as she pulled the boat into the cove again. She had barely gone a minute when she saw Inspector Rawling's boat heading for her. Jumping off the boat, she headed for the caves. She could easily disappear in there. Throwing the rucksack over her shoulder, she ran to the mouth of the cave and skidded to a halt as several rocks came flying down in front of her, barely missing her head. Terrance jumped from the larger of the two boulders down to the sand and stood in front of her.

Secrets and Skeletons In The Teashop

She gasped, "Terrence!" and turned to look back, hearing the noise of Inspector Rawling's boat engine coming tearing into the Cove. Panic in her eyes, she turned back to him.

"How about we split this fifty-fifty?" She held up the rucksack.

"To be sure, the inspector will never find us in the caves."

Terrance's eyes narrowed. He had a plan that would need perfect timing.

"What makes you think I want to make a deal with you?"

"Oh, come on now, Terrance. We both know we are the same, you and me."

A rancid smile pulled at the side of her mouth. Terrance's upper lip twitched, the only movement in his expression as he stared at her. He flicked his eyes past her down to the shore. Inspector Rawlings and his men were running full pelt towards them. He lunged forward and pulled the bag from Patricia's shoulder, swinging it back and over his own shoulder.

"I don't make deals with the devil!"

She screamed in desperation, "Terrance!"

He backed towards the cave, not taking his eyes off her. Inspector Rawlings was about ten feet away. He smiled. Patricia was finally about to get her just desserts, and he was sorry he was about to miss it as Inspector Rawlings placed a hand on her shoulder, and he disappeared into the depths of the cave.

Chapter Thirty-Eight:
Elizabeth

Daniel was pouring out the tea as Faye came down the stairs and into the kitchen.

"Auntie Faye! I've just made us a light breakfast."

Faye looked at the plates piled high with sausages, eggs, bacon, and extra toast that Daniel was putting out on a plate. The kitchen was a mess, with pots and pans scattered everywhere.

"Have you been up for long, cooking?" she said, sitting down.

"I couldn't sleep! I had nightmares about a crazy woman and a madman with a gun. Oh, no. Wait. That was yesterday!"

Faye laughed. "It sounds absurd when you say it like that."

He took a rounded knife from the drawer and put it next to the butter.

"It was more than absurd. It was downright ... well…" he put the frying pan down on the stove and turned to look at her. "Just please promise me that you will never put yourself in harm's way again."

Faye picked up her fork and put a slice of bacon on her plate. "You make it sound like I did it on purpose!"

The doorbell buzzed, and Daniel sighed. "Whoever it is, I'm telling them we're not at home today!"

She smiled. He was a comfort, which she needed right now. Gwen followed Daniel back into the kitchen.

Secrets and Skeletons In The Teashop

"I've made an exception for Gwen. Just this time."

Gwen gasped. "What's happened in here? It looks like a bomb has gone off!"

"It's just a light breakfast," he snorted.

"Light! You look like you are expecting visitors?"

"No!" he said firmly. "We are not at home for visitors!" Just as the doorbell buzzed again, he threw his hands up in the air in despair and headed to the front door.

Daniel walked back into the kitchen, followed by Inspector Rawlings. Faye's heart jumped at the sight of him. She looked away, hoping he had not seen her staring as Daniel pulled his mouth back in acceptance.

"I've made an exception for Inspector Rawlings as well."

Hat in hand, Inspector Rawlings looked across the table, his eyes meeting Faye's. His stomach twisted into a knot. He wanted to speak with her alone, but this wasn't the time and smiled as she glanced at him and looked away.

"Well, this is a nice spread, Daniel."

"Thank you, inspector." He shot a look at Gwen. "It's nice to be appreciated! Please help yourself."

As Daniel went to sit down, the door buzzed again. "Right! That's it!" He threw down his knife and fork and marched down the hallway to the front door. A few moments later, he walked in sheepishly, his cheeks flushed, followed by Elizabeth Percy. "I've made an exception. Lord and Lady Percy are highly valued clients."

"Darling!" Elizabeth rushed over to Faye, kissing her on both cheeks. I had no idea you were entertaining! I don't want to be a bother."

Daniel sighed. "The more the merrier, that's what I say. Please take a seat, won't you, Elizabeth?"

"Thank you, Daniel. But I was only popping around for a quick chat with Faye." She cast a look around at the full table.

"Inspector Rawlings, Gwen darling," she nodded. "I can see you are busy, Faye. I'll call back another time."

Faye stood up. "Nonsense. You are most welcome. Please take a seat."

Gwen beamed a huge smile at her as Inspector Rawlings pulled out a chair.

"Oh. Well. Just for a minute, darling. I don't want to interrupt anything."

Daniel lifted the teapot and poured her a cup of tea. "Oh, there's nothing to interrupt. We've had more than our fill of excitement over the last few days!" he said and glanced Gwen's way again.

Inspector Rawlings stood up and reached over, piling sausages and bacon onto his plate.

"That reminds me. I wanted to let you all know. I apprehended Patricia this morning."

There was an audible gasp in the room.

"Patricia?!" Daniel said in shock.

Secrets and Skeletons In The Teashop

Faye, still in disbelief, looked over at him. "She survived the storm?"

He nodded. "Yes."

"But how did you know she was still alive?"

He added, taking a slice of toast, "I didn't. My men and I were up before dawn. The boat was ready, and we set off as the sun came up."

He finished piling his plate up with another egg and a few tomatoes.

"As luck would have it, we came across her trying to escape the island by boat."

"Who's boat?" Gwen asked.

"Terrance's. He had a small boat moored on the other side of the island. That's who we were going back for. But it seems Patricia stole his getaway boat."

Daniel stopped eating and looked up.

"So, you have them both in custody? Right?" Which was more of a hopeful statement than a question.

"Unfortunately, not. Terrance got away into the caves."

Seeing the look of concern on Daniel's face, he said,

"But I have posted some of my men on the island to flush him out. I'm confident they'll have him in handcuffs in a few days when hunger and thirst kick in."

Faye caught his eye as he sat back down, and he turned to face her.

Penny Townsend

"I hope you will rest easy now, Miss Lantern."

Blushing, she looked away.

"Thank you, Inspector. I will."

Elizabeth placed her teacup back in the saucer with a chink.

"I can see you are being well cared for here, Faye, and it's a relief to know that you are okay after your terrifying ordeal."

She stood up, and her coat pocket caught on the chair. A letter fell out and dropped to the floor. Faye reached down and picked it up. Holding it out, she saw Elizabeth's eyes well up with tears.

"Oh, Elizabeth, are you okay?"

Elizabeth took the letter from her outstretched hand. "I'm not sure." she glanced at the letter. "I received this in the post from my sister yesterday."

Rather than joy at receiving news from her sister, her face was anxious.

Faye whispered softly. "It wasn't good news?"

"I'm not sure what to make of it." She shook her head. "She talks about coming to visit me, only…"

"Yes?" Daniel urged her as everyone had now stopped eating to listen to her.

"Well. The thing is… she died two years ago!"

The sound of Daniel's knife hitting his plate rang out with a loud clatter.

Secrets and Skeletons In The Teashop

Gwen gasped. "Your dead sister is visiting you?"

He glanced at Gwen and shook his head as Inspector Rawlings stood up, his hand held out towards the letter in Elizabeth's grasp.

"May I?"

She handed the letter to him.

"Is this your sister's handwriting?"

Her head nodded in acknowledgment. "Her handwriting is unmistakable. It's always perfectly formed. She was going to teach calligraphy before she left for America."

"May I ask how she died?"

Elizabeth took a deep breath. "She had diphtheria. It happened so fast."

His eyes scanned the letter, stopping to read the last paragraph. "Your sister mentioned she had something important to tell you," he looked back at her. "Have you any idea what she meant by that?"

Faye noticed a look of fear cross Elizabeth's face as she shrugged. "Not that I can think of?"

She took the letter quickly from him and straightened up.

He looked over at Faye. He didn't want her to be part of any more trouble. Faye smiled at him and stood up.

"Elizabeth, please don't worry. I'm sure there is a perfectly good explanation for the letter."

Penny Townsend

Elizabeth waved her hand unconvincingly as if batting the words away. "Yes, yes. I'm sure there is. Well, it was lovely to see you and," she turned, her gaze taking them all in, "I look forward to greeting all of you at the Manor Ball."

She kissed Faye again on the cheek and left.

"Well," Gwen said in astonishment, breaking the silence left by her departure. "Do you think her sister had a secret, and now someone has found out, and they are going to blackmail the Percys?"

Faye sighed. "We really can't go making those assumptions, Gwen."

But Gwen's mind was already racing. "Maybe they'll turn up at the ball. This is going to get interesting."

Daniel looked at her aghast. "You can put all those ridiculous notions out of your head. It's a ball, not an Agatha Christie novel!"

A broad smile swept across her face, and with a glint in her eye, she said. "Of course. We have all been through enough…… When is the Manor ball again?"

Inspector Rawlings felt a knot tighten in his stomach as Faye turned to him and said. "It looks like we've got a mystery on our hands."

Daniel sunk back in his chair.

"Oh, dear Lord……… Here we go again!"

Secrets and Skeletons In The Teashop

Discover more from author

Penny Townsend

Visit www.pennytownsend.com for:

New Book Announcements

*

Book Extracts

*

A Q&A with Penny

And sign up to Penny's newsletter to get the latest updates on her books, find out what she's been up to and be the first to know about exclusive offers and news – scan the QR code below:

Printed in Great Britain
by Amazon